QUIC

Sian M. Williams

QUICKSAND

All rights reserved

Copyright© Sian M. Williams 2020

Cover design by Scow

ISBN: 9798604674413

ACKNOWLEDGEMENTS

With enormous thanks to Suzanne Daniels for her editing, proof reading and wonderful support, and to Gillian Last for her great comments and encouragement.

For all the wonderful people I have met on my travels in the Middle East.

QUICKSAND

Chapter 1

Alan stepped out of the plane into the steaming heat of an Arabian evening in late August. The hot, moist air clamped itself to his hair, his face, his body, and he smiled. The very smell invoked a sense of wealth. He had just had a tender accepted that was worth millions, completed negotiations in less time than expected and managed to get an earlier flight home. As he made his way quickly through passport control, it occurred to him that he hadn't called Barbara to let her know, but he was here now and the chauffeur driven Limousine would be waiting. He bought a bottle of champagne in duty free and made his way quickly to the car. Alan nodded at his driver, Salem, and they set off smoothly down the six-lane highway. He settled back and admired the lush flowering bushes and trees lining the central reservation and roadsides – the result of constant, costly irrigation in the naturally arid landscape. As the car went onto the flyover, the lights of the city spread out before him and reached upwards. Cranes silhouetted the twilight sky signifying the massive construction projects underway as the new city prospered and expanded. Alan gave a sigh of successful well being; he felt pretty good.

Harry fumbled hurriedly with the buttons on Barbara's blouse, then the front clip on her bra and reached for the cascading breasts as his lips fell on her erect nipples. She pushed his undone shirt over his shoulders and pulling the sleeves down over his arms, started on the button of his trousers. As he shook the shirt to the floor, they collapsed onto the sofa. His hands grappled the heavy bosom and then moved down to push her skirt up and pull her pants off. Barbara's hand was now inside his trousers and he paused, breathing heavily, to jump up, remove his lower garments and climb on top of her.

Alan tipped Salem generously and received a huge, grin of yellowing, rotten teeth with large gaps in gratitude. Taking his small suit-carrier and travel bag, Alan made his way into the cool marble entrance hall in his apartment block, a sharp contrast to the heat of the air outside. He whistled as he lightly pushed the button for the lift and waited. The door opened, he stepped aside and smiled as a young Arabic boy rushed past him followed by a Filipino housemaid who called after the boy with shrill, unheeded words. On another day he might have groaned and sworn under his breath at their behaviour, but not today. Nothing could spoil his mood today. He stepped into the lift and pressed fifteen. He glanced at his Rolex and noted that it was eight o'clock.

Plenty of time to shower, change, crack open the champagne and take Barbara out for a celebratory meal. He fancied Japanese. Plenty of sake – get Barbara in the mood and put the finishing touches on a few very good days. He stepped out of the lift.

'Oh God! Oh yes, oh yes!' panted Barbara, as Harry bounced up and down on top of her as she tried very hard to concentrate on her orgasm and not her bottom falling between the cushions. The key went into the keyhole.

'Oh God! Oh shit!' Barbara hissed, climax forgotten as she shoved Harry off into a frustrated heap on the floor. They both scrabbled with clothes. The front door clicked shut.

'Hi! Barbara?'

Alan walked into the living room.

Chapter 2

'Come on Pinter, out you get,' said Rachel as she held the car door open and reached in to grab as many of the ten or so shopping bags as she could manage in one go. It was hot, hot and humid and she felt sticky and uncomfortable. Pinter lazily lolloped onto the pavement and then burst into aggressive life as he spotted a cat perched on the garden wall. He charged, heckles raised, a torrent of loud but ineffectual barks aimed at the impudent tomcat who looked down with disdain, casually slid off the other side of the wall, and disappeared.

'Pinter!'

The dog stopped huffing and snarling and looked sheepishly up, realised it was far too hot for such behaviour and trotted inside the gate to flop in the shade of the eucalyptus tree. Rachel struggled up to the front door, dropped the bags on the step, and rang the bell before returning for the remaining shopping. She pushed the car door shut with her bottom and leaving it unlocked and running went into the villa to find Junata already unpacking and putting the stuff away.

'Ooh, it's hot out there Junata. I'm just off to the school to pick up Lauren and Max. Can you get some burgers out for their lunch, please?'

'Okay madam,' replied the plump, smiling Sri Lankan. Rachel glanced in the mirror on her way back down the hall. She had blotches of mascara on her eyelids and her face glistened with sweat. She quickly rubbed the black smudges away with her finger, pushed her dark, damp fringe back and then let it flop down again as she sighed and shoved on the dark sunglasses to hide behind. As she ran out to the car, she glanced at her watch, ten past one. 'Damn!' she said to herself.

She arrived at the school and managed to find a place to park amidst the normal chaos of cars blocking the road, chauffeur driven cars with blacked out windows double-parked outside the gates. Horns blared as other drivers tried to get past. Mothers and housemaids were already leaving with their children; the mums were all immaculately dressed and looking cool and unflustered. She hurried past, shouting hellos and waving to friends. Lauren saw her coming and shouted, 'Mummy!' as she ran with open arms towards her. She was a thin, petite four-year old with long white blond hair tied back in a bow. Like her father, she always managed to look neat but she had a bubbly, affectionate nature, which Rachel hoped she'd never lose. Struggling behind came Max, socks sagging at his ankles, bag dragging on the floor and shirt hanging out the back. His dark hair stuck up in tufts above a cheeky looking five-year old face. Rachel let go of Lauren and hugged Max, who stiffened and pulled away.

'Come on Superman, let's go get some lunch,' she said brightly, ruffling his hair.

'Get off,' he grumbled, trying not to smile.

'What have we got, what have we got?' yelled Lauren.

'What would you like, what would you like?' Rachel sang back.

'Burgers!' Max put in.

'Yes, burgers!' echoed Lauren.

'We'll just have to wait and see what there is.'

They clambered into the Nissan Patrol and Rachel buckled them in to their car seats. Just as she was walking round to the driver's side, she caught sight of Althea Richter pulling out. Althea wound down her window to shout hello. Rachel waved and called back.

'Welcome back to the madness of school runs! See you at swimming this afternoon?' Althea asked.

'Yes we'll be there.'

'Did you hear about Alan and Barbara?'

'Yes, everyone was talking about it yesterday morning, when I dropped off the children.'

'Isn't it unbelievable!'

'Absolutely incredible,' agreed Rachel. 'Got to go. See you later.'

QUICKSAND

Althea drove off and Rachel climbed into her car.

Barbara and Alan – the rumours had been flying for months. As people returned from their summer holidays, the news had spread like a plague of locusts devouring the juicy facts and passing on the information, stripping bare the reputations of those involved. Another in a long line of affairs and scandal. She shook her head sadly as she drove back home. As they got into the villa, Lauren ran down the hall shouting for Junata.

Max dropped his bag and went to switch on the TV.

'Oh, no you don't – wash your hands and sit at the table,' said Rachel. Max shrugged off to the bathroom just as the phone rang.

'Hello,' Rachel called into the receiver.

'Hello,' came the familiar voice.

'Hello.'

'Hello!'

They both laughed.

'I'm at the airport. Flights been delayed, so I won't be back until ten at the earliest.'

'Oh Martin, what about the party tonight?' She bit her tongue as it came out. She knew it would annoy him.

'Look, I can't exactly help it,' he said, not hiding the irritation.

'No, no, I know you can't. It's okay.'

'You can still go to the party.'

'Yes, I can. Why don't you come there when you get back?'

'Well, I'll see how I feel. Probably be exhausted. It's just one meeting after another and now I've got to sit at the airport for God knows how long.'

'All right. Well, ring me at Kathy's as soon as you get home.'

'Okay. See you later.'

'See you later. Safe Journey.'

Rachel felt deflated. She knew he couldn't help it. It was the job, but it seemed to be that he was away or at meetings, more and more and that she was going out on her own, making excuses for him. She was a very independent person naturally. They both had very separate interests and that suited them, but there were times when it was good to go out as a couple and although she was very capable socially, she hated the inevitable:

'Where's Martin?'

'Oh, he's working. He may come later.'

'It's lucky you're so independent,' said with a pitying look and a tone that always made her feel both martyr like and odd. When she talked to a man, the wife would inevitably appear at his side, charming and friendly but with a very clear message and she would feel amused, but lonely.

She told herself off. He was working hard to pay for

an extremely good lifestyle for them all and Kathy's should be fun. She usually invited interesting people and the food would be out of this world.

Kathy was one of her closest friends, about ten years older she was young at heart, completely down to earth and loved having fun. One of her hobbies was meeting new people and inviting them to dinner where she would indulge in her main love, cooking and entertaining. She always laughed at Rachel, whose attempts at dinner parties involved panic attacks and desperate pleas to Kathy to help at the last minute. It was just a lack of confidence. She was a great cook and growing up she had done practically all the cooking for the family, but the thought of entertaining a crowd filled her with dread.

Rachel smiled as she thought about her last disastrous effort when she was still breastfeeding Lauren. The beef Wellington had actually turned out beautifully, but as she'd removed it from the oven using a tea towel, she'd burnt her hand, dropped the roasting tin and seen her beautiful creation disintegrate on the kitchen floor. Kathy had rushed to the rescue citing the three-second rule for allowing food to be on the floor. Through tears, she and Kathy had quickly salvaged the pieces and put it back together like a badly fitting jigsaw puzzle. After that, she refused to cook for dinner parties preferring to invite the local Indian take-away round for catering when they decided it was their turn to entertain and now that they lived in a villa, barbeques were a much easier option.

She dialled Kathy's office number where she worked as manager of a recruitment service. She was extremely efficient and well respected despite having a hangover most mornings. Kathy had been there for the birth of both Lauren and Max and acted as surrogate grandmother. Rachel's own mother had died when Rachel was eleven years old, leaving her father to bring up three children alone.

'Hi Kathy, it's Rachel.'

'Hello, how are you? Listen, can I call you back?'

'Just a quickie, Martin won't be able to make it tonight so it'll just be me – is that okay?'

'Not a problem – come about eight.'

'Great, shall I bring anything?'

'Just yourself will do. By the way did you hear about Alan and Barbara Wilson?'

'Yes I did, everyone's talking about it.'

'Another one bites the dust. Incredible isn't it? Anyway, can't stop now – got to go, I've got someone here. Bye!'

Rachel put the phone down and it rang again. It was Jane, a midwife at the local maternity hospital. They had become friends when Rachel and Martin first arrived, child-free days when they had lived it up night after night, struggled through the day with hangovers and started again the next evening. Dancing the night away on a Thursday at the disco on the Fourteenth floor of one of the hotels and staying there for the free breakfast they served at four in the morning. In fact, Rachel and Martin still went out three or four times a week, the social calendar always seemed to be full, but Rachel had stopped going out so late when the children were tiny. Jane couldn't really understand why Rachel wasn't so much fun anymore, but they stayed friends.

She met up with Jane whenever she could and they talked for hours on the phone. Or at least, Jane talked. She had the ability to make conversation out of changing the bed sheets, would give you a list of her activities from the moment she got up and her plans for the rest of that day and week and occasionally remember to ask Rachel what she'd been doing. It had become a standing joke between them. Martin would walk into the room to find Rachel with the phone balanced between head and shoulder sorting out a cupboard or making a meal and offering the odd 'yes', 'good', 'mmm', and he'd shout 'Hi Jane!' and he'd be right every time.

This time she was unbelievably brief, 'Rachel, it's Jane.'

'How are you?'

'I'm fine, well no, I'm not fine. Could I meet you for lunch tomorrow?'

'Yes, of course, but not until just after twelve, I'll come straight after work. I'll have to get back in time to take Lauren and Max to swimming lessons, though.'

'Okay, I'll see you at the Italian in the Sheraton at twelve-fifteen. Thanks and bye for now.'

'Jane, Jane?' But she had gone.

'Odd,' thought Rachel, and then decided Jane had probably had an argument with Peter and needed a good session slagging him off before going home and making up again. She smiled. She and Jane had both used each other in this way. They would go for long walks along the beach with their dogs, laze in the clear, blue water, say whatever was on their minds, and offer little bits of advice, though none was really necessary. It was just the need to say things, to stop them whirling around in the head until they whipped up into a cyclone and came out in a torrent of anger and destruction, with their husbands meeting the eye of the storm.

Using each other as sounding boards, situations became clearer, less traumatic and marriage threatening. They would lie on the warm sand and move onto what they were going to wear to the next dinner dance, how much weight they'd lost or put on and who was having an affair with whom.

It was a small town; everybody knew everybody else's business or if they didn't they made it up. Any bit of gossip or speculation was pounced upon, ravaged and passed on with exaggeration at the next coffee morning or dinner party, in the bar or by the pool. Thousands of western expatriates with lifestyles that allowed an extensive social life. Many men had finished work by three and many women had part time jobs or didn't work at all and employed housemaids to cook, clean and baby-sit. Many ordinary people suddenly found themselves enjoying reasonable affluence with time on their hands.

Here there was almost permanent sunshine; when it got too hot, as it did in the summer months, there was air conditioning and chilled pools. You could sail, dive, play tennis, netball, hockey, rugby, even golf on sand or on the new superb grass course that had opened in the neighbouring city. The list of activities was endless and all had a strong social element attached. For the majority, money was not a problem.

Chapter 3

Rachel was a highly qualified secretary working in London as PA to a lawyer when she met Martin at an incredibly stuffy party. Someone introduced them and she started talking to him out of politeness. He seemed a lot older, she was twenty and most of her friends seemed young and immature in comparison to him. It turned out that he was twenty-six and already doing well in the world of banking and finance. As they talked she realised her first impression of staidness was completely wrong. Every so often, he would say something incredibly funny, but so subtle that she had to look at him to check it was intentional and there, at the edge of his rather sexy, deep, dark eyes, had been a little crinkle of a smile. A give away on his otherwise straight face. She liked him and when he invited her to dinner, she had accepted.

It had been a slow, gentle courtship. She was wary about falling in love. It had been nearly two years since she had broken up with Jack and although it was well and truly over, the wounds were still open. She'd been hopelessly, desperately in love. In her confident, unscathed innocence, she had opened her heart and loved with total trust and abandonment. He had loved her in return and it had been a wild, passionate, all-encompassing relationship. They did everything together, saw each other every single day and had so much fun. She thought that they would be together forever.

Then things went wrong. After 'A' levels, he had gone to university and she had gone to secretarial college, both in different cities. They had been sure that they could make it work and at first, they met up every weekend. Then he started to make excuses about why it wasn't possible. He started to back off, wanted more space, wasn't ready to settle down. She thought he was the 'one', but she was wrong. He finished with her and left her distraught.

For months, she put on a happy face, while her body felt it was going to cave in, collapse into a jelly like substance and disappear through a crack in the floor. For months, she woke with her stomach at the back of her throat, her body yearning for the touch of his hand on her skin and the smell of him next to her. With time, it faded and her thoughts became clearer. The memories still painful, she moved into an understanding that it wasn't her, wasn't him just the wrong time. First love. She emerged stronger with a heightened sense of self-preservation. Slightly more cynical, but luckily not bitter, she found herself, a woman more sensitive and aware of other people's feelings.

She went out with a number of men afterwards – all casual, fun and had remained friends with most of them. She found she enjoyed men's company and valued their friendship. Martin was warm, trusting, and solid. She insisted on keeping up her own interests and he had his own.

His main passion was sailing and he often took her down to the coast where he kept a boat at his brother's beach house. He'd tried to teach her the basics, but she suffered dreadfully from sea-sickness and insisted he go on his own while she stayed on the beach, sunbathing, swimming, if the weather was good enough, going for walks along the beach, reading or painting. She knew Martin appreciated this. He enjoyed his brother's company and together they became totally absorbed in manoeuvring the small Kestrel across the waves, working with the wind to build up greater and greater speed to fly across the water, the rougher the better. They came back windswept, salty and exhilarated. In the evening, the three of them wandered up to the local pub for a bar meal and copious beers. They discussed everything. Martin with his rigid, set ideas on things and Rachel earnestly trying to show him a different point of view. Then she noticed his eyes crinkling at the edges, and laughed in exasperation when he said, 'You know I'm always right.'

Back in London, she went to play squash or to see a film or a show with her girl friends and he stayed in or maybe went out for a couple of beers with his friends. He hated cinemas and theatres but never minded her going. She fell in love with the freedom he gave her and the freedom she could give him. He didn't make her heart beat wildly or her knees go to jelly, but she felt comfortable. Sometimes she craved more affection and more demonstrations of his feelings and then, out of the blue, he bought her flowers or a surprise present and she filled with warmth. She decided that this was what a mature relationship should be like and began to think that maybe it was time that they moved in together.

One Saturday during lunch at their favourite Greek restaurant, he told her about his promotion. She screamed with delight and ordered a bottle of champagne. He'd meant to say more but she announced it to the whole restaurant. The Greek musicians started playing some celebratory music, the waiters started dancing and before they knew it everybody in the small place was up and dancing round the room. Rachel and Martin left at four, laughing and high on Retsina, champagne and Metaxas. Hardly noticing the bitter cold, they ran back to Martin's flat, fell in the door and began making love in the hallway.

Laughing and kissing, they undressed each other, clumsily giggling and fumbling as they made their way to the bedroom leaving a trail of clothes. They made love and slept alternately until the following lunchtime when hunger and thirst finally drove them to the kitchen. They took the huge tray of pate, cheese, salad and pickled onions back to bed and Rachel insisted they watch the Sunday matinee, a romantic comedy. As it finished, she sighed and snuggled up to Martin's strong smooth chest, gently running her finger down from one nipple, across his navel and back up to the other nipple.

He groaned as the blood began to surge once more with desire. Then he gently laid his hand on hers and began to tell her that this promotion would mean travelling abroad.

'That's great,' she murmured.

'I don't just mean trips abroad,' he started. 'I mean they will want me to go on a sort of permanent basis to work in their branches overseas.'

'Oh, I see,' she replied with a small lump of fear beginning to form. 'How long would you have to go for?' she asked casually.

'Well, I'd be on three year postings with forty-five days leave each year.'

'Oh, I see,' she said again, the lump growing, her defences rising.

'So I thought that maybe we should get married.'

Slowly she raised her eyes and looked up at him. He looked at her; there were no crinkles at the edge of his eyes. He looked boyish and shy. It was the first time she'd ever seen him not in control, not completely sure of himself and she felt a deep shock within her as she realised how much she loved him, how good she felt with him; safe and secure.

'Well I think maybe you're right,' she said softly.

He slid down to face her and holding her pretty face in his hands, he kissed her, gently at first and then more passionately as she kissed him back. His hand moved down to her full, smooth breast and her nipples hardened and rose. His hand went down her back and along her thigh as his lips moved down her neck and on to first one breast and then the other, licking, teasing the taut buds. She moaned softly as he moved down and she was lost, engulfed in sensations of pure pleasure as his tongue probed and taunted until she pulled him desperately up and into her. Later, with the freezing wind rattling the windows, they sat and talked about where the bank would send him, how much money he would be earning and, she pointed out, what she would be able to do. Working was important to her. She was very good at her job, paid very highly and got a great deal of satisfaction working so closely to the hub of the country's government. A total scatterbrain at home, she was efficient and organised at work.

They planned an August wedding, he would go out to wherever, find a place to live and suss out the work situation for her.

When they discovered it was the Middle East, she panicked. There would be nothing for her to do, she would become a 'wife' having to hold coffee mornings and talk Tupperware. Martin managed to make her wait and see and on his first trip away, he had woken her with a call at midnight.

'Hello Rachey!' His voice sounded slightly slurred.

'Martin, it's midnight!'

'Oh, oh are you sure, it's four here, oh damn I thought it was eight o'clock in the morning, for you.' he laughed.

'Martin, you sound terrible, you've been drinking,' she laughed and then she thought, 'Oh God he's been drinking some methylated spirit concoction!' She'd heard about people brewing their own and how you could go blind or be poisoned. 'What have you been doing? Why are you out so late?'

'Rache, Rache, you'll love it here. There are loads of things to do, a great social life, really welcoming, friendly people. Weather is glorious, it's a bit hot at the moment but it gets cooler – oh, and you'll have no problem finding work.'

And so, they enjoyed an excellent wedding day with Martin looking tanned, fit and handsome and Rachel glowing with happiness in a cream strapless silk dress, with an overskirt that flowed and swirled romantically around her ankles. When it was time to leave, she put on a matching short jacket and then tore off the overskirt to reveal long shapely legs under a very short cream leather skirt. Their friends roared as she threw the men the overskirt and the girls her bouquet while Aunty Harriet put her hand to her mouth in horror and her Dad smiled and shook his head with a glistening tear in his eye. Then they were off, off to the airport and on a plane to the Middle East.

Chapter 4

It took Alan a couple of seconds to register the sight before his eyes. Harry had managed somehow to get his trousers on and finished pulling on his shirt as Alan entered. Barbara had sat up pulling her skirt down and had managed to get her blouse on. Not daring to turn around she did up her buttons. Alan's stomach flipped over and he could feel the colour drain from his face.

'I think you'd better go,' he said calmly to Harry. His face wild with panic, Harry fumbled hurriedly with the buttons on his shirt and slipped on his shoes. He glanced at Barbara who nodded for him to go and, gratefully, he rushed out of the room and the flat. Alan in the meantime had gone to the bar to pour two large brandies. When he heard the door slam, he turned towards Barbara who sat with her eyes looking down. He handed her a glass, sat in the armchair opposite and took a large sip. The silence stretched between them.

Finally, Alan spoke, 'Why?' he asked.

She looked up at this and burst into tears. He waited until she had regained control enough to start talking, between sobs, 'You, you went off with Gina,' she stated as she leaned forward to take a tissue from the box on the side table, wiped her eyes and blew her nose.

'But we sorted that out, it was two years ago. It meant nothing,' he said.

'For you it was sorted out. Oh yes. I took you back and everything was wonderful for a while. Then you forgot about it and went back to working and working. But I didn't forget, couldn't forget. I tried, believe me, I tried, but it ate away at me. And every time you phoned to say you'd be late, every time you went away on business I would start to think well, if you've done it once, you'll do it again.'

'Oh, no! I have been working hard for us, for the children, to give you everything, to make up for – you know.'

'Money – yes I have beautiful clothes, I drive a Mercedes, you have your Porsche. I have enough gold to make Fort Knox seem empty. Regular facials, manicures, pedicures. Holidays in five star hotels – it's wonderful. There's no shortage of money.'

'But I swear I haven't ever... not since.'

'It doesn't make any difference. In fact, deep down I believe you wouldn't, but well, Harry started paying me attention a few weeks ago and it was nice and then one night we got drunk and things happened and I thought why the hell not? We haven't actually, well you know, before. Tonight was the first time we...'

'Did you have to bring him here? What about the

children for God's sake!'

'They're sleeping over at Bella's.'

'Do you love him?'

She looked up at him, her eyes red, 'No, I don't love him. I love you!'

She started to cry again and he came over and took her in his arms and cried with her.

'I'm sorry. I'm sorry,' he whispered, rocking her and stroking her hair.

'I'm sorry. I'm sorry,' she returned.

They stayed up all night talking things through. Talking about their life, life in the Middle East, and made plans for their future, together. Barbara said she would go back to the UK with the children to avoid the inevitable scandal while Alan gave in his notice and applied for a job elsewhere. Somewhere they could try to start again.

Harry went straight to the pub and confided in a friend who in turn confided in a couple of friends who all went home and told their wives and girlfriends. Within twenty-four hours, it was hot gossip across town and the story had changed at least as many times.

Chapter 5

Rachel sat in the cool lounge sipping a gin and tonic. The children were in bed and there was silence apart from the hum of the air conditioning unit. She put her head back on the sofa and closed her eyes enjoying the peace, enjoying stopping after a long, hectic day.

She was up at six-thirty on school days followed by the usual mad panic to get the children up and off to school for seven-thirty. At the office by eight to deal with Abdullah's appointments, flights, paper work, and hopefully finishing at midday to give her time to do some shopping or other errands before collecting the children. Then in the afternoons she ran the children to their various activities, round to friends' houses or to the Club for a swim and a run around and home for tea, bath, bedtime and out somewhere with Martin, if he was home.

She had been lucky with this job. When they had first arrived, eight years ago now, there hadn't been the choice of work she'd hoped for. She'd done some temping in boring offices for very little money and split shifts from eight to twelve and then back in from four to six in the evening. She hated those shifts, but they both enjoyed the lifestyle. She missed the theatre and culture, and although things were improving slowly, she got very frustrated watching pirate copies of films with unclear pictures and terrible sound quality. On the TV, she could watch CNN, The Bold and the Beautiful or camel racing.

However, she played in a squash league, joined a hockey club and had even been given a role in a local choral group production. Martin had of course joined the sailing club and learnt to scuba dive. They'd had an excellent time going to parties, out for dinner, camping trips in the desert, out on speed boats or just lazing at the expat Club. When Max and then Lauren came along, she gave up working to look after them. Time had flown with sleepless nights and Martin working hard, but Junata enabled them to keep up their hobbies and they still had a good social life.

Martin had been very successful at the bank and was now regional manager. The initial three years were extended indefinitely, and they moved from an apartment into a villa. Of course, the promotion meant far greater responsibility and travel to meetings at other banks in the region. Although she had a full time housemaid, pregnancy and small children had taken something from her. A piece of her brain had gone missing, she functioned on intellectual half steam in order to cope with the emotional demands of young babies without losing her mind altogether. She had struggled to lose the weight she had put on and with

Martin stressed out with work she felt like she had turned into a breeding cow with no real identity.

When Lauren started school, she began to realise she could look around again, notice that the sky was blue and that she was still a thinking, attractive woman with her own emotional needs. She decided to go back to work. Martin didn't really see the need. They had enough money and he found it slightly amusing that she needed her own identity, a feeling of independence and something that was hers.

When she started, he was slightly patronising, teasing her about the 'mickey mouse' job from eight to twelve. She ignored his comments, though they left a small wound deep inside, and she began to find herself again. She was respected for her efficiency and organisational skills, popular with the important Arab bosses, and with the low paid, hard-working Indian typists and tea boys. She gained an insight into the very different mentalities of different cultures and learnt to play them at their own game rather than getting frustrated because they didn't do things the British way.

At work she was Rachel Drummond, not Lauren and Max's mum or Martin's wife and although it was not as stimulating or demanding as her work in London, it was better than lazing round the pool or going to coffee mornings. She sat vaguely thinking about how time had passed. They had been there for eight years. She had been working for a year now. Martin not coming back on time irked her. It suddenly seemed a long time since they'd really done anything together.

She felt a strange loneliness sitting in their beautifully furnished lounge.

She finished her drink and looked at the antique carriage clock on the sideboard, a wedding present from her old boss in London. It kept perfect time and announced with a clear chime that it was quarter to eight.

'Oh shit!' she said aloud.

'Sorry, madam,' came Junata's sing song voice from behind her, 'You going out tonight?'

Rachel laughed, 'Yes, I'm going out Junata. Martin should be home about ten. I'm going to Kathy's house – shouldn't be late.'

'You go Kathy's – always late,' she admonished.

'No I don't think so; I'm shattered. Shock to the system starting the school run again – anyway I'd better get ready if I'm going to go at all.'

Junata walked away nodding her head from side to side knowingly.

Rachel stepped into the shower and quickly washed her hair. She glanced down at her legs and realised she was well overdue for a shave. 'Damn!' she said as she looked for a razor and remembered she had left the new packet downstairs.

'Oh well, that makes what to wear a bit easier.'

She was out and dry in a couple of minutes, pulling on a clean pair of pants followed by a bra that should have been white but had a grey tinge to it. She didn't spend much time buying clothes anymore, there were no decent shopping malls, but she tried to remind herself to get new underwear. When had she stopped caring about her appearance?

She took out her trusted black trousers and did them up while she looked for a suitable top. Quickly, she threw a royal blue silk blouse with a scoop neck and short sleeves over her head and tucked it in. It felt loose and cool against her skin. Then she remembered deodorant, and had to carefully hold the material away from her as she ran the roll on under her arms and waited a couple of seconds for it to dry. She frowned as she thought about what Martin would say if he'd been there to watch her.

'For God's sake Rache, think about what you're doing!'

'Well sod him,' she thought, 'He isn't here.'

She tucked herself in and looked in the mirror. Her shoulder length dark hair stuck out in tufts and she'd got damp patches on the shoulders of her shirt. She rubbed her head brusquely with a towel and combed it through. Hurriedly, she put on a touch of eyeliner and mascara and put lipstick in her pocket to put on in the car. She gave her hair, and shoulders a quick blast with the hair dryer and was thankful that she'd finally taken the plunge a year ago and had her very long, thick, dark hair cut shorter. Maybe even shorter would be better. She pulled the fringe down with her fingers – shrugged at herself in the mirror and slipped her feet into black, low-heeled shoes. She ran downstairs, grabbed a bottle of wine from the rack and put it into a plastic shopping bag. It wasn't done to be seen carrying a bottle in the street, even if alcohol was allowed for those with a liquor licence. She picked up the car keys and called 'bye' to Junata as she went out of the door. It was twenty past eight. The wave of hot air outside wrapped itself around her, moist and clammy.

Quickly turning on the engine to get the air-conditioning blowing, she turned up the radio as she set off across town. An old Carole King record, 'It's Too Late', was playing and she sang along. Suddenly, she jammed on her brakes as a taxi pulled up directly in front of her without any indication. 'You bastard!' she muttered. As she overtook it, she glared at the driver, an Asian with dark expressionless eyes, a long full beard and dingy length of material wrapped around his head. He did not look at her but made the gesture of shaking two fingers closed on thumb, the usual reaction meaning, 'Just be patient'.

In the fifteen-minute journey across town, she was cut up twice; stuck behind an Arab in a Mercedes on his car phone weaving to the left and right, and nearly crushed by a bus whose driver decided to turn right but hadn't bothered to check whether there was anything in the right hand lane. A fairly uneventful journey by normal standards.

She drove past Burger Queen and Kentucky Fried Chicken and the row of small shops selling cheap plastic shoes, imitation polo and lacrosse shirts and pirated cassette tapes. The street thronged with men in white dish-dash. A cluster of women covered from head to toe moved together like a black amoeba across the road, heedless of cars. Indians and Sri Lankans in brightly coloured saris sauntered along between the cross section of nationalities in a mixture of European and Eastern dress. While the taxi drivers hooted incessantly, people moved slowly, leisurely between the high, modern buildings. It was too hot to rush.

Rachel drove behind the main street onto sandy tracks that had not yet been turned into proper roads, parked and made her way into the nineteen-storey block. It was a new building and the marble steps and lobby were shiny and cool. The lift moved quickly without a sound up to the tenth floor and within seconds, she was standing before the door of Kathy's flat ready to ring the bell. A sudden knot of fear formed itself in her stomach and she felt incredibly self-conscious. She tried to look at herself in the brass doorframe but could only see an elongated blur of features.

'Damn!' she muttered. She'd even forgotten to put on her lipstick in the car. She knew she would be all right once she got talking to a few people but walking into places, that first entrance, filled her with dread.

'Oh why did I come, why didn't I just stay home and wait for Martin?' she asked herself.

She rang the bell. Kathy's husband George opened the door. He was short and plump with a bald shiny head and a bulbous red nose. When he saw Rachel, his face broke into a wide smile and his blue eyes sparkled.

He always reminded Rachel of a happy, smiling garden gnome.

'Come in, come in, we're all waiting for you.'

'Oh, I'm sorry, am I late George?' she kissed him and handed over the bottle.

'Well, a few people have died from starvation in the corner but they weren't very good company anyway.'

He led her into the spacious, elegantly designed lounge where about thirty people of ages ranging from mid-twenties to sixty were standing in small groups or sitting chatting and laughing. There was a relaxed charm about the room, age had no relevance. Kathy as usual, had managed to ensure an atmosphere of ease and warmth. Rachel fixed a smile on her face, but was unable to focus on anyone in particular and take in who was there. Kathy's large exuberant voice reached her.

'Rachel, great, you made it. Get one of the waiters to get you a drink and I'll introduce you to some people. There's champagne if you want some.'

Rachel nodded to one of the waiters from the Club. 'I'll have a wine and soda please, Hisham.'

The tall, thin Indian grinned and went off. Rachel needed to go to the bathroom. She had convinced herself that her mascara was smudged over half her face and that nobody was going to tell her.

'Kathy, I've got to go to the loo – hang on a second.'

She exited and getting into the toilet, locked the

door and rushed to the mirror. She looked fine. She put on some honey rose lipstick, a soft natural looking colour which accentuated her full lips, told herself to pull herself together and with a deep breath she went back into the lounge. She saw Eleanor Stevens on the other side of the room with her husband Dave and gave her a wave. Eleanor was a tall, thin lady in her mid-thirties. She had a pointed, bird like face and her hair and make-up were immaculate. She wore a beautifully tailored peach trouser suit with a cream blouse. She held a wine glass in the long slender fingers of one hand and held a cigarette in the other, displaying pale orange manicured nails. Her husband was a good looking, characterless man with smooth dark hair and a tall lean frame. He looked like a male model in his high-waisted casual trousers, shirt with perfectly rolled sleeves, top button open and loafers without socks.

'Good clothes, attractive body, but no personality,' thought Rachel.

Hisham brought Rachel her drink and she moved to join the small group of people around Kathy. Michael and Janet Bright she already knew. Michael was an amusing man in his mid-forties. He worked for one of the oil companies, earned a good salary and enjoyed life. He came from the East End, had a strong cockney accent and was proud of the fact that he was a working class lad made good. Janet was a mean faced, moaning gossip who enjoyed his salary, but seemed to find enjoying life a bit difficult. She wore numerous gold chains around her neck, three or four diamond rings adorned little fat fingers and heavy gold hoops hung from her ears. She was wearing black leggings and a sparkling sequined top, which came to the top of a protruding gut, which a nip and tuck operation had failed to remove, but which she failed to notice. She wore high stiletto shoes, which brought her up to five feet four and her over bleached hair sat dry and stiff above an over made up face. The other couple, Rachel vaguely recognised but didn't know.

Richard and Gillian Bright were Scottish. He was ginger and serious looking but laughed easily at Michael's anecdotes while Gillian was dark haired and pale skinned with a bubbly laugh. Both were in their mid thirties. They had been in town for just three months and Kathy had taken them under her wing after Gillian had come into the recruiting agency looking for work. Kathy introduced them and moved away.

'So where's Martin?' asked the mealy mouthed Janet.

'Oh he's been held up, should be coming along later though,' replied Rachel brightly.

'You're very brave coming on your own,' added Janet.

'Not really, it's better than sitting, waiting at home,' Rachel tried to keep the annoyance out of her voice.

'He'd better watch himself, that Martin,' interrupted Michael. 'Letting such a gorgeous bird out on her own, I might have to run off with you myself,' he laughed, a deep throaty roar and put his arm around her.

'I don't suppose I have any say in the matter, tweet, tweet,' retorted Rachel and he hugged her again and laughed.

Gillian and Richard laughed with them and Janet's lips pressed together in a thin smile.

'Did Kathy manage to find you a job, Gillian?' asked Rachel, turning away from Michael.

'Yes, I start working on Sunday as a kindergarten teacher.'

'Oh, good for you, I could never do that, two of my own at home is enough!'

They continued to talk and discovering that they both played squash agreed to arrange a game sometime the following week. Rachel began to relax; trust Kathy to introduce her to someone she knew she'd get on with.

Kathy invited everyone to start eating and led the way through to the dining room where a sumptuous array of food lay on the table for people to help themselves. Smoked salmon with caviar, oysters and king prawns, cold ham, chicken pâté and numerous salads were there for starters, beef stroganoff, chicken with cashew and vegetable moussaka lay in casserole dishes on burners. There was French bread, Arabic pitta bread and plates with hummus and tabbouleh on the side board; chocolate mousse, lemon soufflé and a vast cheeseboard next to an over laden fruit bowl. Rachel filled a plate and looked for a place to sit down. She loved eating and the food was mouth-watering, but she always found eating off her lap very difficult to do elegantly so she tried to find a discreet corner in which to enjoy without embarrassing herself.

Going back through to the lounge she found a camel stool next to the window and sat down half facing the room and half looking out of the full length glass. Sitting so close to the glass she could see beyond the reflections of the people in the room out onto the busy Corniche and out across the beautifully calm sea; it was inky black with the occasional boat sending red and white flashes across the water. The hum of chatter mixed with the heady beat of the background music contrasted with the silent movement of matchbox traffic below.

Balancing the plate on her knees, she cut into a succulent piece of ham and raised it on her fork. Before she reached her mouth, she looked up and caught sight of a man she had never seen before. The fork automatically continued on its path into her mouth; she closed her mouth and withdrew the implement, her teeth slowly moved into action and she chewed and swallowed. He was tall, very fit looking with wavy, slightly wild dark hair.

'Hi Rachel!' Rachel looked up to see Nick Philips pulling up a chair next to her.

'Nick!' she said, always pleased to see her good friend from the choral group. He was a maths teacher, slim and tall with only a very fine covering of short, prematurely grey hair preventing him from being completely bald. He had a kind face and soft, brown eyes. He sat down with his plate of food, and looked down at her perched on the low camel stool and laughed. 'What are you doing down there?' He asked and bent to kiss her on both cheeks.

'There's less distance for my food to fall from here,' she laughed.

'Haven't seen you for ages. What have you been doing with yourself?'

'Oh I don't know, working, running after the children.'

'You getting involved with the next production?'

'Well, I got the letter. Auditions are next week aren't they?'

'Yes, you should go – we miss your dulcet tones and your sense of humour.'

'Thank you, I don't know though' Rachel replied.

She was tempted but knew that the commitment for a show took up a great deal of time and nervous energy. She looked out of the window. It was over five years since she had had an actual part in a show. She had continued to support the group and helped backstage with make-up and costumes. Maybe it was time to get fully involved again.

'Hello Nick.'

'Oh, hi Gary.'

Rachel looked round to see the tall, fit looking man with wild, wavy hair looking down at her.

'Gary, this is Rachel.'

Gary held out his hand and she took it. He held it firmly, briefly and said hello.

'Hello' she said in a clear, friendly voice looking straight into his blue eyes.

He smiled and his whole face smiled, with his full lips and long, straight nose. He rested easily on the arm of the settee beside her, holding a pint of beer. She could not explain the unreasonable effect he was having on her. The touch of his hand had sent a strange sensation right through her body. She was aware of his close proximity and when his calf brushed against her knee, she felt an inexplicable shock and an inability or reluctance to move her leg away.

'I was just trying to persuade Rachel to go for a part in the next choral group production. She's got a fabulous voice.'

'Bit out of practice, I'm afraid,' said Rachel modestly.

'Gary here is going to be stage manager.'

'Oh, is that right? Have you done anything before?'

'Well I got involved with the drama group in Brunei when we were living there.'

Rachel finished the remaining salad on her plate. At the 'we' she had felt a strange twang of disappointment. He went on to explain that he was an engineer and enjoyed getting involved with set designing and painting, had worked backstage on the last show and thought he'd give stage management a go.

Rachel told him how nervous she had been the last time she had been involved. It had been her first time on stage since playing Tweedle Dee in a school production of 'Alice through the Looking Glass'.

'The time has come' the Walrus said, 'To talk of many things!' began Gary.

'Of shoes and ships and sealing wax – of cabbages and kings' Rachel continued and then paused, 'Oh, what comes next? Something about the sea and pigs having wings,' she laughed excitedly. 'God, I must read it to Max and Lauren. I love it.'

'Can I get either of you a drink?' interrupted Nick.

'Oh thanks, Nick. I'll have a wine and soda,' said Rachel.

'I'll have a lager,' added Gary.

'Right, I'll see if I can find a waiter.' Nick picked up his plate and offered to take Rachel's.

'Oh, thank you. I must go and try some of that lemon soufflé in a minute. It's my absolute favourite of favourite foods.'

Nick set off across the room to the bar.

'Who are Max and Lauren?' Gary enquired casually.

'Oh, my children. Lauren is four and Max is five. Have you got any?'

'Yes, two; Jody is nine and Paul is eleven next

week,' he paused, then went on, 'Do you work?'

'Of sorts, I've got a job as a PA to the Arabic boss of a trading company.' Rachel found herself telling him about the job, how important it was for her to work and yet compared to the work she'd had in London it was totally unsatisfying.

She found herself saying things she'd never even admitted to herself, not wanting the dissatisfaction to creep in and upset the balance of her life with Martin and the children. He didn't ask the normal question, 'What does your husband do?' and she immediately liked him for that.

Nick returned with the drinks, 'Sorry I got caught at the bar' he said. Neither Rachel nor Gary had noticed he'd been a long time, but Rachel realised Nick had been cut out of the conversation and thanking him for the drink began talking to him about the choral group. The three of them retold anecdotes of disasters they remembered from previous involvements with amateur productions.

The party was livening up. In the middle of the room, people were starting to dance to sixties and seventies music; Kathy was in the middle twisting – her large frame wobbling uncontrollably under the loose kaftan she was wearing. Opposite her was one of her colleagues; a greying sober looking man in daylight hours, he had now discarded jacket and tie and was waving his arms in the air while his large gut bobbed over the edge of his belt. Eleanor and Dave were attempting to jive and a young woman was wiggling her slim hips provocatively in front of her awkward, rhythm free husband. A group of men standing at the side drinking and smoking unashamedly watched her cleavage dangerously close to bouncing free of the tight lycra dress she was just wearing. Rachel caught Gary's eyes and they both smiled.

A tall, long legged lady made her way across the room. She had long, wavy, white blonde hair and the most beautiful face. Wearing jeans and a plain white T-shirt she looked like a Scandinavian model for Timotei shampoo. 'She would have played Alice' thought Rachel. She was stepping carefully, a glass of wine in one slender hand. As she passed the group of men they forgot the escaping bosom and stared at her appreciatively, one of them asking, 'Who's that?' and the other pointing at Gary and saying something.

Rachel watched her come up to them, a little unsteadily. She smiled sweetly at Rachel and settled herself onto Gary's leg; his arm went round her waist. Again, Rachel felt the twang, but gave a huge smile and said, 'Hello!'

'Nina, this is Rachel and you've met Nick before.'

'Hi, Nick!' she waved her glass at him 'And hello Rachel, pleased to meet you.' She moved her glass into her left hand and held out the right to shake hands. A long elegant hand with long red nails, she shook Rachel's hand in a firm grip.

She finished the wine in her glass in one gulp and turned her face to Gary's, 'I think I've had too much to drink. Will you take me home?' She kissed him softly on the cheek.

Rachel took a sip of her drink.

'Yeah, okay,' said Gary without a trace of reluctance. He finished his drink and they stood up. Gary took his glass and Nina's to the bar and returned, 'See you soon,' he said to Rachel and Nick with a broad grin.

'Nice to meet you,' said Nina.

'And you,' replied Rachel with a smile.

Gary led Nina over to say good-bye to Kathy and George with a strong arm around her waist. Rachel watched them briefly and turned to Nick, 'He's very nice isn't he? And she's absolutely stunning.'

'Is she?' He said with a straight face then smiled cheekily.

'As if you hadn't noticed,' she hit his arm laughing.

'He's ex SAS,' said Nick, 'Not going to mess with him!'

'Ah, I thought he looked fit,' said Rachel.

Nick raised an eyebrow at her.

'Strong, I mean strong,' Rachel said, laughing. 'Come on, do you fancy a dance?'

They both got up to join in with the Time Warp. Rachel felt a strange mixture of elation and deflation, but not allowing herself to think she threw herself into the fast moving dance steps and at the end, exhausted and laughing, gave Nick a hug and went over to the bar to get a soda water. Janet Bright was telling Althea Richter a 'highly confidential' story in a loud, slurred voice, Althea pretended she had not heard it before.

'Oh, yes she's definitely been having an affair.'

'Are you sure, she and Alan seem so close?'

'Oh yes that's all for show. They're having real problems and she's been seeing Harry for over a year now.'

'No!'

'Yes, it all came out last week so Alan is sending her and the kids back to the UK.'

'Well, what's Harry going to do?'

'Nobody seems to know, but it's Alan I feel sorry for.'

Rachel took her soda and moved away. It was of course the hottest story in town at the moment. The fact that 'poor Alan' had had an affair two years previously seemed to have been forgotten. She glanced at the clock on the wall and thought, 'Oh shit' as she realised it was nearly one in the morning. She went to find Kathy who was sitting in an armchair, glass of wine in one hand, cigarette in the other, her smooth, rosy cheeks glistening.

'Rachel! Where have you been?'

'Oh, talking, dancing, enjoying myself.'

'Good, that's all right then.'

'And now I'm going home.'

'Oh Rachel, one more drink for the road.'

'I'd love to Kathy, but I've got to get up for work.'

'So have we all.'

'I know, but my old body can't cope with no sleep anymore.'

'Old, You're not even thirty yet – come on.' Kathy bent forward, about to get up.

'No, stay where you are. Thank you, it's been excellent – as always. Save me some lemon soufflé will you, I didn't get round to having any,' Rachel grinned.

'If you can't stay and eat it now, then don't think I'll save you any,' returned Kathy.

'Thanks Kathy – I'll call you tomorrow.' She bent to kiss her.

'Gary's nice, isn't he?' Kathy said.

'Yes he is and his wife's fabulous,' Rachel replied innocently.

'Give my love to Martin,' Kathy added and smiled mischievously. 'Tell him what he missed.'

'Bye Kathy.' Rachel kissed her and said good-bye to George and let herself out.

As she stood, waiting for the lift, the music and chatter hummed and thudded behind the door. She stepped into the empty lift and felt suddenly, very lonely. Martin had not phoned.

Driving back across town, the roads now quiet, the memory of Gary's leg touching hers came back to her, followed by the sight of him walking away with his arm around Nina and she wanted Martin. Badly.

Letting herself quietly into the sleeping house, Pinter greeted her by wagging his whole body and nuzzling into her. 'Hello boy, good boy,' she ruffled his coat and hugged him. Seemingly satisfied, he went back to his basket at the foot of the stairs and turning around three times flopped down, watching her until she went up the stairs and switched off the light. With a contented snuffle, he laid his head on his paws and slept. His family was home.

She undressed quickly, washed her face, brushed her teeth in the children's bathroom and went through to her own bedroom. She crept into her side of the bed and reached across to touch Martin's smooth shoulder. He grunted but didn't move. She snuggled up to his back and kissed the smooth skin. He turned, still half asleep, and put his arm around her. She kissed him gently on the lips, he twitched and murmured and then rolled over turning his back to her and let out the low reverberant snore of deep sleep. Rachel held her hand down between her legs and heady and tired, also fell asleep.

She walked across the green field. On either side were tall trees. It was sunny and blue. A man stood at the far end of the field and she walked towards him but the field seemed to stretch out in front of her further and further and then she was there but the man had gone. A beautiful butterfly fluttered onto the sand so she dived into the clear water and swam with ease and strength up towards the sunlight shining through the surface, up and up she must get up.

'Mummy, wake up, wake up!'

Rachel opened her eyes, still aware of the vivid dream; she looked into the face of Lauren.

'Hello darling,' she smiled and pulled her into bed with her.

She was fully awake now – a good morning person – and once awake she was ready to jump up and face the world. She checked the clock – it was quarter past seven. She had forgotten to set the alarm. She panicked before remembering that it was Thursday and the children didn't have school. Good old Junata had got the children up and had sent Lauren in to wake her. She shoved Lauren out of bed and looked at Martin still fast asleep. Leaving him there, knowing he probably wasn't planning on going in until later, she went through to shower and dress.

Chapter 6

After a quick cup of coffee and a piece of toast, she made sure the children were settled and told them that Lorraine, the mother of a boy in Max's class was going to pick them up to go to the park and that she would see them later. The air was thick with humidity and she could feel pricks of sweat on her face as she got into her car to drive to the office. The DJ on the radio, a very funny young man from up North, was regaling a story about the night before, carefully avoiding the mention of any hotel and referring to alcohol as grape juice or refreshments. He had been banned on numerous occasions for saying the wrong thing. He played very close to the edge with cryptic allusions to people living in the city and what they had been getting up to and chose records that summed up whatever he was referring to, so that everyone knew what he meant. He dedicated a record to his friend, Harry, 'When I Grow Up' by the Beach Boys. Rachel couldn't help smiling as the words 'Ba-ba-ba-ba Barbara-Ann,' came over the air.

Most of the road near to the office block she worked in was a mass of dug up sand, tractors and trucks. Hordes of Indian and Pakistani workers digging and carrying in temperatures that reached over forty degrees centigrade at mid-day seemed undaunted by the heat. Rachel managed to find a parking space about one hundred metres from the entrance and even that distance at eight in the morning meant she would be uncomfortably warm by the time she got into the office. As she was about to open the glass door to the building, she heard someone call her name behind her. Turning, her heart gave an unexpected leap as she recognised Gary coming up the steps behind her.

She smiled and said, 'Hello.'

'Good morning, Tweedledee!'

She laughed remembering the conversation the night before.

'How are you this morning?' he continued.

'Not too bad, so far. I wasn't that late leaving.'

'What are you doing in my building?' he asked.

'This is my building actually,' she said with mocking.

'Well, why are you standing outside then?'

He went forward and held the door open for her. As she went through with a 'thank you,' she touched against him and felt again the almost tangible sensation. They shared the lift talking about Kathy and how they both knew her. As Rachel stepped out at the fifth floor, he said, 'See you at the auditions next Tuesday.'

'Oh, maybe, yes, bye.'

The lift doors closed to take him up to the sixteenth floor. Rachel had noticed the button he'd pressed, as you do when you're in a lift with other people. She vaguely wondered why she had never bumped into him before, went into the office strangely shaky and called for Raju. The small, skinny Indian came slowly along the corridor.

'Morning, Mrs. Rachel.'

'Hi Raju, how are you?'

He wobbled his head from side to side.

'Can you get me a coffee Raju, please – are there any messages?'

'Two people calling, madam.'

'Yes, who Raju?'

Again, he wobbled his head from side to side, 'I am not knowing; they say they call back.'

Rachel shook her head laughing, 'Raju if someone calls, please ask them their name.'

He went off down the corridor with a smile and came back ten minutes later with the coffee. Rachel was sorting through the post on her desk. 'Thanks Raju – quick as a flash as usual,' she raised her eyebrow at him.

'You happy today, Mrs. Rachel – you have good party last night?'

'Yes, thanks Raju – now can you photocopy this pile of papers here. Three copies of each one. Three, okay?' she said smiling.

She sat back to drink her coffee. She did feel happy and strangely excited. She didn't have time to think about it as the phone rang and she was down to business arranging appointments and stalling people she knew Abdullah did not want to see or deal with, giving instructions to department managers and their secretaries. By eleven, her desk was clear and she waited for her boss to make his usual elevenish appearance so she could go through things with him. She telephoned Kathy and thanked her for the party. The last guests had left at four and Kathy said she felt like shit. Rachel laughed and told her it served her right, rubbing it in by telling her that she felt fine. Kathy asked after Martin and Rachel said she hadn't spoken to him yet.

'Give him my love then and we'll see you soon,' finished Kathy.

'Yes, I will. Maybe, see you over the weekend, bye.' As Rachel put down the phone she felt a slight edge of guilt as she realised she hadn't thought about Martin all morning. Now as she did, she remembered with discomfort that he hadn't bothered to phone her at Kathy's when he got back. She dialled his office and left a message with the officious secretary, who told her briskly that Mr. Drummond was in a meeting.

Just before midday, Abdullah arrived. He walked slowly, never hurried, his crisp white kandura swaying as he walked, his white head dress and black banded gutra balanced perfectly around his head with the incongruous gold pen clipped to a top pocket. He had a handsome face, dark skinned with such brown eyes they were nearly black, a long slightly beaked nose, a neatly trimmed customary beard and moustache. He commanded respect, as did most influential Arabs. Rachel was never sure if it was the association with vast wealth developed in a relatively short lucky history or their natural ability to control people's time. Abdullah would deliberately keep someone waiting for hours, even days before making a decision or signing a document and yet when he wanted to, he could make things happen almost immediately. It was this knowledge that led to frustrated, irate managers or salesmen desperately trying to keep cool knowing he would prolong their agony with almost sadistic pleasure, if they showed any impatience. It was a very effective technique.

'Good morning Mrs. Rachel,' he spoke with a slightly Arabic guttural accent. His English was perfect but he deliberately retained the Arabic sound so that when it suited he could fake misunderstanding.

'You look beautiful today.'

'So do you,' she replied. It was totally out of order for a woman to refer to a man's appearance but the first time she had done it, in total naivety, he had been wholly amused and so it had become a standing joke between them.

He snapped his fingers at Raju, who scuttled off to

make Arabic coffee, and went into his office indicating that Rachel should follow. He sat in the leather swivel chair behind the huge, mahogany desk that was bare apart from a telephone and a clean ashtray. The office was huge with a large Persian carpet covering the space between the door and the desk. High backed turquoise and silver armchairs lined the sides of the room and the desk, with two more leather chairs in front of it, sat in front of a large window looking out over a municipal garden, lush and green, to the twinkling sea.

Rachel waited until Abdullah had his coffee pot and small Arabic handle-less cups set before him before going through his business. He listened while he sipped and then when she'd finished and started going through documents to sign he responded as usual. Some he signed, others he handed brusquely back saying,

'No, this can wait.'

'This man is stupid, maybe tomorrow I will sign.'

'What is this?' and she explained.

'Ah, Insh'allah, Insh'allah,' Meaning God willing or, more precisely, that he hadn't made a decision yet and had no intention of doing so for a while. Then he reached for his telephone, which was usually the sign for her to go.

She got up to leave but he signalled with his hands for her to sit down again and then spoke into the phone in fast, loud Arabic. He put the phone down and told her that he was expecting guests for lunch and could she deal with the caterers when they arrived. She groaned inwardly but smiled and said of course.

The caterers arrived half an hour later and she showed them to the room adjacent to Abdullah's office. A huge picture of the President adorned one wall and a luxurious deep pile, turquoise carpet covered the floor. There were two rows of four stately chairs in cream with gold braid lining two walls but otherwise no furniture. The two Pakistani caterers unrolled a plastic sheet and laid it across the middle of the floor before setting out piles of pitta bread, plastic containers with hummus, tabbouleh, kufta, falafel and one large platter of lamb and rice. When the guests arrived, they would sit cross legged around the sheet eating with their hands while they discussed business.

Rachel went back to her desk, checked all the signed documents in the out tray and put the others in a file with notes on who to phone the next day. Then, saying good-bye to Raju, she left the office. She wondered vaguely if she would see Gary and then switched to thinking about meeting Jane for lunch, getting something for dinner and getting the children to their swimming lesson.

Chapter 7

She rushed into Mario's ten minutes late. Jane was sitting at a table with a drink and looking at her watch pointedly.

'I'm sorry. Got held up at work.'

'Don't worry,' Jane said, 'What do you want to drink?'

'I'll have a soda water, thanks.'

'Is that all? Heavy night last night?'

'Actually no, I was very restrained. I'm just hot and thirsty at the moment – we'll have some wine with the meal, shall we?'

'Right you are,' said Jane as she caught the attention of a waitress.

A sulky faced Filipino girl came to the table, took the order in an offhand manner and handed them both a menu. Rachel thanked her and smiled but it was not reciprocated. Jane and Rachel looked at each other and laughed. They both began to peruse the menus but

Rachel couldn't concentrate. She looked over at Jane, who was studying the menu as if it was a cryptic crossword puzzle and said, 'So come on then, tell me what this is all about. You sounded desperate on the phone yesterday.'

'Let's order and then I'll tell you,' replied Jane. Rachel smiled, it was typical of Jane to build up the suspense. She loved to make a drama out of anything that happened. She looked down at the menu of Italian salads, antipasti, pasta and pizza dishes and decided on tagliatelle with a special seafood sauce.

Glancing round the room, which was light and sunny in the daytime, she took in the red and white checked tablecloths on the ten or so tables of varying sizes. The chairs were wicker and wine bottle candle holders with dried red wax from deliberately dripped candles stood unlit ready to create a warm genial atmosphere in the evenings. Usually quiet at lunchtime, it was a bubbling, lively place at night with a fast turnover. A constant stream of pizzas and pasta dishes would be delivered accompanied by the shouts of orders and the cries of the chef in temperamental Italian fashion, which had made him a personality and added to the popularity of the restaurant.

Four businessmen sat at one window table consuming large quantities of wine, talking loudly; a middle-aged couple sat in a corner talking quietly and sporadically. The only other customer was a distinguished looking man, with silver-grey receding hair, eating carefully, totally engrossed in his meal without looking up in fear of catching someone's eye, a veneer of being quite comfortable dining alone.

The waitress brought an appetizer of bruschetta, finely chopped tomato and onion in balsamic vinegar on a small piece of toast, and took their order. Rachel ate the offering with pleasure and looked up at Jane who had not touched hers.

'It's delicious, don't you want yours?' asked Rachel hopefully. Jane said she didn't fancy it, so Rachel happily ate that too.

'That's not like you,' Rachel said wiping the crumbs from the corner of her mouth with the napkin.

'It's all right for you,' said Jane. 'You never put on weight.'

Rachel looked up in surprise and then laughed. Jane was slim and small. She had a delicate frame, and dainty feminine hands, which Rachel had always envied. She tried to gauge the expression on Jane's extremely pretty, girlish face. She had naturally blonde, naturally curly hair, which framed her lightly tanned face, beautifully setting off the big blue eyes, small slightly upturned nose and sensuous mouth. She was thirty-five, but looked twenty-five.

'What on earth is the matter? People would die for a figure like yours.'

'Yes, but I'm going to put on weight, and more weight and I'll look ridiculous at my height.'

'Put on weight, but why? Oh!' it suddenly dawned

on her. 'Are you pregnant?' she asked in a hushed, shocked voice.

'Yes,' and with that the blue eyes filled with tears, which tipped over and began to roll.

'That's wonderful!' Rachel laughed and clapped her hands with glee. 'Oh I can't believe it,' and she laughed again.

Jane could not help but laugh too. With tears falling, she laughed and spluttered, reaching for a tissue in her bag.

'It's not funny,' she said blowing her nose. 'I'll get all fat and Peter will hate it, and I won't know what to do with a baby.'

'Of course you will. Aren't you pleased at all?'

'No, well yes, but I just feel sick and hungry all the time. I cannot see what makes people want more than one, if this is what it's like.'

'Well, how many weeks are you?'

'Oh, about nine apparently.'

'Don't you know?'

'Well, it wasn't planned. I was on the pill, I had that awful stomach bug. Then I started feeling a bit odd and then throwing up. I thought I'd got some terminal disease, so I went to the doctor. She suggested pregnancy and I told her I couldn't be. Anyway, she said she'd do a test just to eliminate the possibility and of course, I was. I felt so stupid, I'm a midwife for God's sake, and then horrified. I couldn't even remember when I'd had a period, so she did a scan and we both agreed it was about eight weeks. I've not stopped crying since.'

'What does Peter say?'

'I haven't told him.'

'What! Why not?'

'I'm afraid he'll be angry and well, though I'm upset, I feel sort of excited and that it's meant to be, do you know what I mean?'

'Yes, yes, I do, but I'm sure he'll feel the same – you've got to tell him or he will be upset.'

'I know, I will, I'll tell him tonight.'

The waitress set down the bowls of creamy pasta and poured out two glasses from the carafe of wine.

'Well cheers!' said Rachel raising her glass. 'I think its excellent news, and I'm sure Peter will too.'

'Cheers, thank you. I suppose I shouldn't drink any more – but well, what the hell.'

They both laughed and started eating heartily, despite Jane's protestations of feeling sick. Rachel found herself thinking about how she'd felt during both her pregnancies. She had been lucky with both children. They had been carefully planned, healthy pregnancies ending in normal deliveries. Max had been born nine days late after eight hours and Lauren had arrived a week early after six hours of labour. She'd had nausea, backache, heartburn and with Lauren terrible headaches and constipation, but these were of course to be expected and nothing to worry about or so she was told at her antenatal classes. The episiotomy had meant sitting in salt baths and feeding while she sat on a foam ring for the first four weeks, but compared to what some women went through she'd had an easy time. She remembered the 'friends' who had related their own horrific stories with relish as soon as she'd found out that she was pregnant and moved into this special circle of mothers or mothers to be. She had vowed she would not do the same but although she avoided frightening tales, she found that it was like welcoming a new member into a secret club that could not be shared by or explained to men or women who had not had a baby.

As a midwife, Jane was surprisingly naïve about pregnancy. She knew all the practicalities and was well aware of horrible possibilities, which added to her fear, but it had always been somehow impersonal, her job. No one can ever teach you the real effect of hormonal changes on a personality; the inner turmoil caused by this small being growing inside you acting as an emotional catalyst. The struggle sometimes to remain balanced because you are physically healthy and having a baby is natural. Having finally told someone, Jane talked incessantly about how she felt, when the baby was due and how that would fit in with work and whether or not she should give up work altogether.

They paid the bill and made their way to the car park. Rachel gave Jane a hug and congratulated her once more, telling her to let her know how Peter reacted. Feeling slightly light headed after the wine she drove home smiling at Jane's dramatic reaction.

Chapter 8

She arrived at the Club, an expatriate leisure complex of which many of the British community and a few other nationalities were members and left the car by the tennis courts. The sailing club was busy with members preparing their boats for the afternoon race. The crews launched kestrels and lasers into the channel and made their way to the start point. Rachel looked for Martin, knowing that he would be there getting ready to go, but couldn't see him. Privately owned power boats of varying sizes were parked on the other side of the slipway.

Max ran on ahead while Lauren held Rachel's hand, past the tennis and netball courts, the indoor sports complex and up onto the pool deck, which overlooked the beach area. She got Lauren and Max changed and joined three other mothers at the shallow end of the pool. Althea Richter was relating the story she'd heard the night before to Sylvia Burroughs and Mary Watson. They'd all heard varying versions of the scenario and each was adding some extra vital piece of information to the picture. Apparently, Alan had actually caught Barbara in bed with Harry. In his own bed. Gasp! He'd come back early and the children were both on sleepovers at friends. How stupid of her to do it in her own flat. She's going back to the UK. Flying tonight. Poor Alan.

'How did the children take it?' Rachel asked. The three women looked at her and Mary said, 'Well no one seems to know. Of course it must be terribly upsetting being taken out of the country in such a rush and at the beginning of the school year.'

The others all nodded in agreement. They moved on to discuss other relationships that had fallen by the wayside due to affairs. Dennis and Maureen Jones; Maureen had run off with her tennis coach. Ian and Freda Lettfast; Ian had left her for a Thai girl he'd met on a golfing holiday. Apparently, she was now pregnant and he would be a father again at the age of fifty-eight.

Rachel called a waiter over, ordered some coffee, and asked if any of them wanted a drink. With the subject interrupted, they began to discuss how hot it was for the time of year and how well their children were doing at swimming. Rachel turned to Mary, a chubby, buxom woman with long straight mousy hair, and asked her if she was going to the choral group auditions. She had a plump, smooth face with quite large, brown, doe-like eyes. She had a beautiful singing voice and was used to getting the leading roles, even though she didn't always look quite right for the parts.

'Oh I don't know. Nick Philips is directing and I'm not sure that he's really up to it.'

'Nick's directing? He didn't tell me that. Good for him. I'm sure he'll be great,' said Rachel.

'Well, he knows his stuff but I don't know if he'll be strong enough and I'm not sure if I've got the time,' said Mary dismissively.

'Oh, but you've got such a beautiful voice,' Rachel said, knowing this was what Mary wanted to hear.

'Yes,' said Sylvia. "The voice of an angel. You have to be in it, Mary. I love to hear you sing.'

'Mmm, thank you, well, we'll see.' Mary replied smugly.

'Give us a tune now and we'll see which part would suit you,' said Althea. She began singing 'Happy Talking' very badly and everyone laughed.

'What about you Rachel?' asked Althea, 'I've heard you've got a lovely voice.'

'I'm thinking about it, actually,' said Rachel. 'Might be fun.'

'Oh yes, you should,' said Mary, not quite convincingly.

Sylvia cut in, 'I really admire anybody who can get up on stage. Doing the props is as close as I'll get, plus the fact that I've got a voice like a cat on heat. Not quite as bad as Althea, but bad enough.'

Althea feigned upset and they all laughed. Sylvia

was a thin Mancunian. She had pulled her fine, dark hair back from her face in a tight ponytail. She had large, bright eyes like a tiny rodent whose eyes stared out constantly on the watch for predators. She smoked one cigarette after the other and never seemed to be quite still even when there was no body part moving. With her droll northern dialect, she often put herself down with a funny quip at her own expense or someone else's. She was kind and generous but a constant worrier.

'How's Charlotte?' asked Rachel. Charlotte was Sylvia's youngest. She was now eight months old; the other two children, Ben and James were seven and eight. Charlotte had been a surprise pregnancy and Sylvia had suffered badly from post-natal depression.

'Oh, she's okay. I've left her with the maid, but only for an hour. I don't like to leave her for longer than that.'

'Relax, Sylvia it won't do her any harm to be left,' put in Althea, leaning back in her chair and sipping tea.

'Well, yes I know.' Sylvia fidgeted, 'But I'm still breast feeding and she needs me.'

'Are you still feeding?' asked Rachel, surprised.

'Yes, well it's the best thing for them isn't it?'

'Not if it's draining you. Sylvia, you look great, but you have lost a lot of weight.' Mary started. 'You need to get her onto the bottle and then other people can look after the baby without you worrying and losing sleep.' She spoke in a commanding, brusque voice. As far as she could see it was quite obvious what Sylvia should do.

A look of utter despair flicked across Sylvia's face and then she laughed and said, 'Yeah you're right, it's about time Jim found out the difference between her mouth and her arse.'

The slightly rising tension was dissipated as they all laughed and there was a flurry of yelping and shouting as the children ran up with demands for ice cream and crisps and drinks. They were shining, wet and cool as the sun beat down and Rachel used a towel to mop the sweat off her face and sunglasses. She gave Max and Lauren some money and decided she needed a swim. Gently she lowered herself into the refreshingly chilled water. She swam a slow, steady stroke, dodging shouting and laughing children, parents playing with youngsters, young babies happy and gurgling – accustomed to water from a very early age. The few empty sun beds lining the pool filled as people avoiding the mid-day heat arrived. Bodies lay splayed, exposed to the sun. Groups sat talking, drinking and laughing while waiters hurried back and forth taking and delivering orders. A slight breeze brought welcome relief from the oppressive September heat. It was Thursday, start of the weekend.

She swam a couple of leisurely lengths and pulled herself out of the water. Max and Lauren were sitting quietly absorbed in their ice-creams. Sylvia had left in a hurry it seemed, as she'd left a pair of swimming trunks. They lay, small wet and abandoned on the astro turf. Rachel picked them up, checked that they didn't belong to Althea or Mary and said she'd take them round.

Chapter 9

Rachel called in at the supermarket on the way home to get a few bits and pieces. Just popping in to buy a couple of things meant half a trolley full and Max and Lauren begging for sweets and biscuits all the way round.

Getting back into the car, she decided to go via Sylvia's and return the swimming trunks as she would probably need them the following day. Jim and Sylvia lived in a five storey block of flats quite near the supermarket. It was one of the older blocks that had not yet been picked out for demolition to make way for a modern twenty or thirty floor building as the city became higher and denser year by year. There were a few small shops on the ground floor; tatty, overcrowded general stores. The entrance to the building was dim and repugnant, carrying the smell of curry and bad body odour. Some small boys wearing long dish-dash, dark haired, with large dark eyes, played on the steps and stared as she went past holding Max and Lauren's hands.

Stepping out of the cranking claustrophobic lift, she could hear a baby crying. As they moved towards the door of Sylvia's flat, the sound became louder, more insistent. She rang the bell. Max and Lauren stood by her, unusually silent, as she waited. There was no answer but the now almost monotonous wail continued unabated. She pressed the bell again leaning her finger down for a little longer and waited. Rachel began to feel uneasy.

'Can we go home now?' said Lauren.

'Hang on' said Rachel wondering what she should do when the door suddenly opened. Sylvia's face appeared with an annoyed enquiring expression and then changed instantly into a bright smile as she recognised Rachel.

'Oh hello!' she said.

The baby's crying continued.

'Would you like to come in?'

She opened the door and ushered them in, 'It's a bit of a mess but never mind.'

She was incredibly cheerful and welcoming. Rachel followed her in.

'I just popped by to give you Ben's swimming trunks – you left them by the pool – sorry to disturb you.'

Rachel was oddly disconcerted by the friendly welcome. They went into the living room. In complete contrast to the exterior of the building, the flat was large, light and immaculate. Not a toy, a book, or even a newspaper was in sight. Every surface was clean and clear. The chairs were plumped up, cushions were carefully placed, ornaments on the sideboard and shelves lay posed, precisely set. The baby's screaming from a room off the lounge rose in pitch.

Rachel looked at Sylvia who said, 'Would you like a cup of tea?'

'Er, no, don't worry,' said Rachel, 'I think I can hear the baby.'

She sounded ridiculous to herself. Sylvia's face formed a small frown and she cocked her head as though listening for some distant sound and said, 'Oh yes, excuse me.' She left the room and came back cuddling the sobbing child and cooing to it.

'Hush there, shush, hush now.' She sat on one of the chairs and put the baby to her breast where in seconds it was suckling greedily. She looked up at Rachel, 'Sorry I can't offer you a cup of tea,' she said, smiling. She seemed to have forgotten that she had just offered her one.

'No, no don't worry. Would you like me to make you one?' asked Rachel.

'I'm fine, thanks,' replied Sylvia.

'Where are Jim and the boys?' Rachel asked very casually.

'Oh Jim's not home yet and the boys are in their room, watching TV I expect.'

Rachel told Max and Lauren to go and join the boys and then said to Sylvia that she would make a cup of tea. Sylvia looked slightly uncomfortable but once again smiled very brightly and said, 'Sure, you know where everything is.'

Rachel went through to the small, compact windowless kitchen. Everything was away in cupboards, or neatly stacked. It was clean and sparkling. Rachel hadn't wanted to stay – if anything she wanted to get out as quickly as possible – but something told her she should. She went back through with two cups of tea. The baby was sleeping now with a contented look upon its sweet, chubby face.

'Your maid does a great job,' said Rachel looking round the neat room.

'Oh, I don't have a full-time maid,' Sylvia said. 'Only for the odd baby-sitting. I do all the cleaning.'

'Well, the place looks amazing. My house is always a tip even with a maid. The children's things are always everywhere,' Rachel said lightly.

'Oh well I don't work, so I have plenty of time.' She moved the now sleeping Charlotte onto the corner of the settee and put a blanket over her. 'Thank you for making the tea, sorry I couldn't do it.'

She sat on the edge of the chair looking slightly restless. Rachel drank her tea quickly, making small talk. Every so often Sylvia would run her finger through her hair, pushing it back behind her ear and then the finger would move to her mouth and down to her cup. Her sharp eyes would hold Rachel's for a second and then flit to another object somewhere in the room as she responded. Rachel finished and put down her cup and said she'd better be going. She went to the door and called Max and Lauren. There was no response so she went down the corridor and poked her head round the door. The four children were glued to the television watching cartoons.

'Come on you two.'

'Oh, Mum can't we watch a bit more!' cried Lauren.

'No, it's time for supper and bed. It's getting late.'

With general moaning, Max and Lauren rose and moved backwards to the door.

'Say good-bye.'

'Good-bye,' they dutifully chorused. The two boys glanced round and mumbled good-byes before returning their eyes to the set.

Returning to the lounge Sylvia had not moved.

'Are you okay?' asked Rachel.

Sylvia jumped up, suddenly active. Picked up Rachel's cup and said, 'Oh yeah, I'm right as rain – sorry I'm just a bit tired, think I must have a cold coming.'

She laughed nervously.

'Listen, why don't you come round one afternoon with all the children. We've got the garden so they can play outside,' suggested Rachel.

'Oh, that would be lovely, thank you. Yes, we'll do that.'

'Right, well how about next Wednesday?'

'Okay, yes I think that would be fine.'

'Good, thank you for the cup of tea.'

'Thank you for bringing the swimming trunks. That was really thoughtful.'

'Not at all, well, if I don't see you before, I'll see you next Wednesday about two. Okay?'

'Okay, bye,' Sylvia called from the door as Rachel and the children got into the lift.

Chapter 10

Max and Lauren were raving about the cartoons all the way home. Rachel thought over the whole visit. She felt uncomfortable, but couldn't really explain why.

She put it out of her mind as she rushed to get the children sorted and herself ready for going out. Martin came back later than normal, already squiffy from a few beers after sailing and they hurried to get out of the house on time to meet some friends at a popular French bistro.

On the way home, after a lovely meal and a fair amount of wine, she tried to tell Martin about Sylvia but he was very dismissive.

'Think how often you left Lauren and Max to cry. Sometimes you have to just leave them.'

'I know but it was as if she didn't know the baby was crying.'

'Oh, come on Rache, all women with babies get distracted. Remember the time you put your tampons in the freezer and got so upset when you couldn't find them because you were positive you'd bought some?'

'Well I had,' she replied laughing, and then serious again, 'And the house, well it was too tidy.'

'You don't know what too tidy is,' he said. 'I think you've forgotten what it would be like living in the UK with a young family and no help. There are plenty of people who manage without a maid. My mother brought up two boys with my father away most of the week up in the city.'

'Oh God, here we go about your mother, don't forget my father.'

'There you are, you've proved my point for me.'

Rachel was silent for a minute then said, 'Yeah, perhaps.'

'You know I'm right,' he said as they arrived back at the villa.

They went in and Rachel asked him if he wanted a nightcap.

'I'm going straight to bed. I'm sailing again in the morning.'

'You don't fancy a bit of hanky panky then?' she smiled moving towards him and putting her arms around his neck.

'Oh, I'm a bit tired and full of pop.'

He smiled at her and gave her a hug and a quick peck on her forehead, before making for the stairs. He turned at the bottom and said, 'Are my spare sailing shoes in the utility room?'

'Yes, they are on the washing machine,' Rachel replied automatically while her heart was doing strange things. She dismissed the feeling of rejection and checked that his shoes were on the washing machine before following Martin upstairs. By the time she had washed and got into bed, he was already snoring lightly.

Rachel lay for a while running through the events of the day and letting her mind wander at will. When she thought of Sylvia she felt a slight discomfort. Martin was probably right, but even so, she decided to make an effort to see her more often. Since she'd gone back to work, she had seen less of Sylvia and yet when Max and Lauren were small they'd spent quite a bit of time together in the mornings.

They'd been two of the few mothers who had stayed when Saddam Hussein invaded Kuwait. The initial panic had meant many wives and children returned to the UK. Many nationalities fled, while others stocked up on water, taped up their windows with masking tape and even had gas masks at the ready. The threat of scud missiles reaching the country filled people with dread. The initial panic calmed and the city became the place for rest and recuperation for the thousands of navy and air personnel who arrived from Britain and America.

It had been an exciting, frightening time as the suspense grew in the months leading up to the actual war. A feeling of living on the edge pervaded the nation; they were close enough to experience the knowledge of fear and death and yet removed. Everyone felt a responsibility to look after and entertain the men and women based there – never sure if they would be needed to fight or not. Around the pool, young fathers, miles away from their own families, took pleasure in taking Max and Lauren, holding them, playing with them. Ten or so Americans had spent Christmas day with them and it had been a wild, happy day only to be followed by the onset of war and the sad death of one of them at the end of January.

Sylvia, along with many other women, had enjoyed herself immensely, going to wild parties on the ships that came in, flirting outrageously with the young fit men. Her quick wit and filthy sense of humour shocked the sensibilities of the well-mannered Americans and amused the British. Neither she nor Rachel could get over the fact that the gorgeous hunks of American male flesh, trained to kill, referred to them both as 'Ma'am' and would do anything to please. It was rumoured of course that Sylvia had taken full advantage of this but she had sworn innocence. Seemed strange to think that it was only eighteen months ago.

This picture of the laughing, naughty Sylvia did not match the woman Rachel had seen today - vague, nervous, too thin and bland. 'God, what childbirth could do to you' she thought and remembered Jane. She wondered what effect it would have on her. Moving backwards through the day, Gary came to her with a distinct stab of pleasure. Dwelling on that pleasure and failing to analyse it she was asleep.

Chapter 11

Rachel was packing beers and sandwiches into Martin's cool box, Max and Lauren were throwing a ball for Pinter and then chasing him around once he'd caught it, screaming with delight as Pinter growled and dodged until he was ready to drop it and wait for the next throw. Martin came into the kitchen with his sports bag packed, whistling and happy, ready for a morning sailing.

'Have you seen my grey shorts?' he asked.

'Which grey shorts?' Rachel replied.

'The ones I wear for sailing.'

'I don't know; in the drawer I expect. Have you looked?'

'Of course I've looked. They're not there.'

'Hang on and I'll go and have a look.'

Rachel ran upstairs, opened the drawer and underneath some T-shirts were the grey shorts. They were new and she hadn't seen them before. She took them down. 'Here you are.'

'Well, where were they?'

'In the drawer.'

'Well, you must have hidden them.'

'Try opening your eyes next time. I've never seen them before, Junata must have put them away. When did you get them?'

'Oh, I bought them at the airport, last week,' he said dismissively. He took them from her and put them in his bag without saying thank you.

The exchange was light but as Rachel handed him his cool box, gave him a kiss and told him to have a good time, she felt like she may as well have been talking to Max. And he did look like a young boy as he grinned, shouted 'bye' to the children, and set off for the sailing club. Max and Lauren raced outside to wave him goodbye.

At nine, Jane rang to see what Rachel and Martin were doing that night. She sounded happy and lively. Rachel said it was Junata's day off so suggested they come round for a barbecue.

'Have you told Peter yet?' asked Rachel.

'Oh yes, of course,' said Jane as if there had never been a problem. 'He's absolutely over the moon, keeps fussing over me, seeing if I'm all right. It's wonderful, best thing that ever happened.'

'That's great!' laughed Rachel, 'Told you it was nothing to worry about.'

'Oh, I knew he'd be pleased and if it's a boy we're going to call him Alexander or maybe George, but if it's a girl we thought of Angela or Christabel. Peter's convinced it's going to be a boy.' She continued while Rachel finished off sandwiches for their trip out on the boat that afternoon. Finally, she rang off saying that they would be round about half past seven. Rachel smiled to herself at Jane's ability to forget about a problem as soon as it had been solved, as if it had never even existed.

After lunch, Rachel drove down with the children and Pinter to meet Martin and then they all went out on the speedboat that they shared with another couple. It was a good arrangement – they shared the costs but took it in turns to go out on it, ensuring it was put to good use without feeling you had to go out every week.

The sky was a clear blue as they sped across the smooth water that reflected shades ranging from clear turquoise to navy depending on the depth. A breeze created by momentum cooled and refreshed them on the short trip to a small island just offshore. Mangrove trees sprouted up, as if growing on the water until they neared and the thin stretch of sand outlining the land became apparent. The roar of the boat declined to a slow chug and as they came to a stop alongside two other boats, the stillness and the heat settled down upon them.

Waving to the ten or so friends already sitting in the water around floating surfboards used as bars, they jumped off and began unloading the cool box, towels and beach toys. The children threw off their life jackets, leapt into the water with Pinter, and ran splashing to join some playmates digging in the sand. The water was lukewarm, barely refreshing but pleasant to sit or loll in, so while the children, covered in sun block, found the energy to run and play, the adults sat bantering gently, drinking beer in the shallow water.

Eleanor Stevens sat cross legged with the water lapping around her middle. She was wearing a stylish high cut bikini. The top half cleverly thrust what small breasts she had upwards and forwards. She had swept her hair up on to the top of her head and held it in place with a brightly coloured band. She was immaculately made-up as always and occasionally she would scoop a little water over her shoulders and chest careful not to let one drop of water near to her face or hair. Sitting in the shallow water next to Eleanor was her husband Dave in swim shorts of a complimentary colour to her suit, he had one knee up, the other leg outstretched and he leant back on one hand while the other held a can. Every so often Eleanor would run her long fingers down his arm affectionately or feed him an olive from the bowl on one of the surfboards.

'Sweet,' thought Rachel.

Althea Richter sat, also in a high cut bikini, revealing large thighs, and a rolling stomach under a huge sagging cleavage. Every so often, a boat would pass pulling a water-skier or children on a huge rubber ring and the incoming waves that slapped with a pathetic sigh on the shore were nothing compared to the effect she had when she rose to fetch more beers from the cool box. Cellulite and stretch marks that seemed to catch the sun shimmered and shook as she strode over the sand unselfconsciously. Her husband Joe sat darkly tanned, with breasts larger than the average teenage girl balanced on a hairy beer gut that seemed to rise and fall as the water covered and uncovered it. Their two children plump and cheerful stood out amongst the other lithe, slim bodies now searching for shells up the beach. There were two other men, who had just started working for Joe in his cargo, haulage business. New out from the UK they looked pale in comparison to the rest of the tanned group. Lennie was a young lad in his early twenties, slightly loud and arrogant, trying to impress and drinking a lot of beer. The other, Neil, was quieter, early thirties with curly brown hair, small brown eyes and a thick moustache.

Martin was on great form. Having won his race that morning he entertained them with a detailed description of the closing stages. His crew, a teacher at one of the secondary schools named Tina, had had to lean out over the edge until her head was actually brushing the water in order to get up the speed to overtake his arch rival just before the line. Tina had been screaming and yelling and just as they'd won, Martin had momentarily let go of the rudder to punch the air in triumph causing her to get a complete ducking before he righted the boat.

Rachel smoothed suntan cream into her face and bare skin, unconsciously noting the number of times 'Tina' was mentioned. She was wearing a simple yellow one-piece, which showed off her slim, athletic body with long tanned legs, yet covered her not quite flat tummy. She looked good without really being aware of it, mistook the appreciative eyes of the men for being critical and quickly sat where the water reached her arm pits before relaxing.

The men moved together discussing cars. The women moved together to discuss hairdressers, the advantages of leg waxing and when they were having their next facial. Rachel was conscious of the fact that that she hadn't indulged in any of those things for years. Then, of course they moved on to give an analysis of Barbara, Alan and Harry. It was easy, brainless communication. Every so often, one or another would go for a short swim out to relieve themselves and return to join in with the next tack of conversation.

When they began to feel red shouldered and prune like, they took a break from the water, put on T-shirts, ate sandwiches and played a brief game of rounders with the children before needing to jump in the water to cool down.

As they packed up to leave in the late afternoon, the two new men were lobster pink, and everyone was merry – what a great life – everyone was relaxed and easy.

Rachel gritted her teeth as they set off back, hoping the sea would remain calm. Often on return journeys the channel would turn into a choppy mass and the boat would lift up and slam down again as it met each wave. The children and Martin loved it but she and Pinter would cling to each other and by the time they got back, she would feel tense and sick totally negating the relaxing afternoon on the beach. Luckily, it was fine.

It wasn't until they were loading up the car that Rachel suddenly remembered to tell Martin that Peter and Jane were coming round.

'For God's sake Rache, why?' Martin said, climbing into the driver's seat.

'Hang on, they wanted us to go out with them and as Junata's off I suggested they came to us.' Rachel said, quietly defensive. She buckled Max into his seat and kissed him on the forehead, before getting into the car herself and pulling the door shut. Martin set off down the road at speed.

'Why do we have to see them at all? I wanted a quiet evening. Why didn't you ask me?'

He was shouting now. Lauren and Max went silent and stared out of the windows.

'There's no need to shout.' Rachel said.

'I will shout, don't patronize me!' he yelled.

'Listen, Jane's pregnant, I expect they want to celebrate – they're our friends.'

'Jane's what?' he had stopped yelling.

'Pregnant.'

'Bloody hell! Thanks for telling me.'

'I did tell you.'

'No, you didn't, you never tell me anything.'

'Well, perhaps that's because you're never here to tell.'

'Oh don't start that.'

'Start what?'

'Having a go at my job.'

Rachel breathed in deeply, 'Look I'm sorry. I should have asked you before telling Jane they could come. Do you want me to ring when we get in and put them off?' As usual, Rachel found herself placating, calming the situation.

'It's a bit late now, isn't it?'

'No, its six now, they're not coming until half seven.'

'Oh and I suppose you'll tell Jane that I don't want them over?'

'I can find an excuse.'

'No, it's too late now, we'll have to let them come.'

The stab wound in Rachel's heart bled a little. They stopped at the supermarket to buy food for the barbeque and by the time Jane and Peter arrived, Martin had showered and changed, the children were in bed, the barbecue was alight and champagne was on ice. He greeted them cheerfully, honestly pleased at their news.

Peter was tall, six-foot four with broad shoulders and short cropped, slightly receding black hair. He was an excellent rugby player and one of the lads but he held a protective arm around Jane's slight shoulders and grinned continuously, the pride on his face shining out. Jane's eyes glistened with love as she basked in his sudden tenderness and allowed him to treat her like some fragile flower. She exchanged a conspiratorial glance with Rachel who wondered cynically how long this it last.

They had a good evening and were just toasting 'Peter Junior' who was going to be a future England prop forward or 'Jane Junior' who would also have to be an England prop forward when the phone rang. Rachel picked it up and spoke gaily into the mouthpiece. It was Joe Richter.

'Rachel. Listen, is Martin there?'

'Yes – What's up Joe?'

'It's Lennie Tyler - he's had a crash.'

'Oh no!' At first Rachel had to wrack her brain to think who Lennie Tyler was. Then she remembered the brash young man at the beach.

'Oh God! Is he all right? What happened?'

'He's broken a couple of ribs and is pretty shaken but the main thing is he hit a cyclist and he'd been drinking, he's in hospital handcuffed to the bed with a police guard. I need to speak to Martin – see if he's got connections at the embassy who can help.'

'Yes of course – hang on.'

She called Martin to the phone, explained briefly and went through to tell Jane and Peter. Suddenly the champagne lost its flavour. They all knew the consequences of having an accident. If you injured or worse killed someone, you had to pay 'diya' or blood money to the family. If drink was involved, he could expect deportation or the possibility of having his head shaved and spending an indefinite period in an appalling prison waiting for the court case. A lot depended on knowing the right people at the embassy.

Nearly everyone drank and drove. Years before it had been easy to get away with. There was less traffic and there were many stories of the police stopping drivers and giving them a lift home, rather than arresting them. The traffic was increasing and the laws were becoming stricter, particularly if anyone was injured in an accident. There was no excuse really, taxis were everywhere and cheaper than getting a bus in the UK, but still a lot of people drove after drinking for hours.

The next day was Saturday. Martin got up but Rachel remained in bed. If Martin was at home, he took the children to school on Saturdays and allowed Rachel an extra hour. She vaguely kissed her husband goodbye, clinging onto sleep or she would wake and be unable to go back again. She drifted back into a light, dreaming doze thinking how thankful she was that they had Junata and wondering how Lennie Tyler was feeling.

Lennie Tyler felt horrendous. His mouth was dry, his head throbbed, and when he had first woken up it had taken a while to remember exactly where he was. Then it had hit him like a punch in the stomach and he felt sick. He had tried to move but the pain in his ribs caused him to groan and keep still. It was then that he also realised that his ankle was chained to the end of the hospital bed. He filled with fear and dread. He prayed to God to get him out of there, out of the country. That country, which only yesterday afternoon basking in the glorious sun in drunken euphoria, he had praised and thanked for allowing him to be there, 'Why had he been so stupid?' Remorse gnawed at his insides as he thought about the job, the money, the opportunities, the life he had ruined.

Behind the scenes contacts had been made, phone calls, a few favours owing and following the news that the cyclist was unhurt, Lennie Tyler was strapped up and flown painfully but expediently back to the UK. He was famous in the bars for one night and then forgotten.

Chapter 12

On Tuesday evening, Rachel left a note for Martin reminding him that she had gone to the choral society auditions. He had flown out on the Sunday and was due back that night. Driving to the Club, she began to feel decidedly nervous. She hoped she wouldn't make a fool of herself. As she locked the car door, Nick Philips walked past.

'Rachel, great! You decided to come then?'

'Yes, well, thought I'd give it a go. Just get a part in the chorus or something small.'

'Well, we'll see about that,' he smiled.

'Of course, you're directing aren't you? Good for you.' Rachel said. She was glad to have someone with whom to walk into the room.

There were about fifteen people already in the hall, most of whom she didn't recognise. Nick introduced her to a few and then went off to talk to the musical director. Mary Watson was at the piano talking to the pianist. She spotted Rachel and gave her a brilliant smile. 'Rachel, glad you could make it!' and turned back to Susan. More people started to arrive and went to the bar to get themselves drinks. Rachel got herself a beer and sat down with a few people she vaguely knew who continued their conversation.

She felt a little lost and looked around. As she did so, she saw Gary walking through the door and her stomach leapt unexpectedly. She became intensely aware of herself and rather than catching his eye and saying hello she found herself turning to the woman next to her and asking her if she had been involved in many productions. The woman launched into a detailed account of her roles in the last three shows and Rachel listened intently or at least she gave the impression of listening. Every sense in her body seemed to have come alive. She was aware of his presence without seeing him and then suddenly he was beside her, saying hello and pulling a chair up and she found herself chatting to him easily, happily, the woman on the other side of her forgotten.

Nick called everyone's attention and explained how the auditions would work. He had chosen a few songs out of the show. Songs that they would all recognise. They'd sing them through together and then those that wanted to go for solo parts would be asked to stand up and sing. Then he would do some readings and again those that wanted main speaking parts would audition up on the stage. A burble of chatter arose as the pianist handed out song sheets and then quiet as she returned to the piano and ran through the introduction to 'Nothing like a Dame.' Gary tapped Rachel lightly and whispered 'Good luck, I'll see you later.' She grinned nervously at him and butterflies fluttered madly in her stomach. She wasn't sure if it was just the auditions creating the sensation. Then she threw herself into the songs along with the thirty or so others there.

Three or four people stood up to sing alone and then she heard Nick call out her name. She suddenly felt sick and wished for a hole in the floor but found herself standing, taking a deep breath and waiting for the intro. Once she started singing, she forgot where she was and, apart from faltering once or twice, sang out clearly and strongly. When she finished, she sat down quickly, everyone clapped politely as they had done for the others. She felt flushed and awkward. She looked at the woman on her left and received a patronizing smile and 'Well done, very nice dear.' She gulped down some beer and caught sight of Gary to her right. He winked discreetly and smiled, a broad encouraging smile, and she shrugged and grimaced back at him.

After the singing, she went up on the stage and read for various different parts with Nick swapping people around and trying different combinations. Mary Watson appeared confident and at ease, interrupting every so often to ask exactly how Nick wanted a particular line to be said. Rachel could tell Nick was irritated but he remained cool and tactful. Finally, everyone was happy that they'd had a go at anything they wanted and the auditions were over. Nick would ring everyone over the next few days to tell them the casting.

Most people started to leave, others went up to the bar. Nick went into a huddle with the musical director and the pianist. A couple of people went past Rachel and complimented her on her voice. She thanked them shyly and felt extremely flattered. Mary Watson joined four or five others at the bar and they closed into a small clique. Rachel picked up her bag and decided to go home. She looked around for Gary but couldn't see him so she headed out towards her car. As she left the hall, she tripped on a step and stumbled forward. A strong hand caught her arm and stopped her from falling.

'Oh shit!' she exclaimed.

'That's a matter of opinion' said Gary.

Rachel laughed and said, 'Sorry, thanks.'

He was still holding her arm and once again, she was aware of the almost tangible link between them. It set her senses whirling and yet at the same time it felt comforting, as if she belonged there, close to him. She looked up into his face and noted honest concern as he asked if she was all right.

'Apart from feeling embarrassed, I think I'm fine' she said. She went to take a step and pain shot through her ankle causing an involuntary yelp to come out.

'Are you sure?' he asked.

She tried her foot again, gingerly and then with more confidence and realised it was okay, just a twinge.

'Come on, come back in and sit down for a bit. I'll

buy you a drink.'

She was about to refuse and then thought 'why not?' He led her back inside to a chair and, though she insisted she was fine, made her sit down. He returned with a brandy for her and a beer for himself. Handing her the glass he said, 'For medicinal purposes.'

'Of course,' she replied with a smile and thanked him.

'You sing beautifully,' he said quite matter of factly.

'Thank you. I do love it, though it's mostly in the car or the shower these days.'

She told him about the band she'd been in at school – all girls, they'd been quite popular at local discos and at friends' parties and had had all sorts of visions of fame and fortune, then 'A' levels had become a priority. Parents had clamped down and after that the band members dispersed to various colleges, universities and jobs.

They talked on, in a separate world, oblivious to other people around them. Finally, Nick interrupted them when he came over to join them. Rachel felt irritated, she liked Nick very much but she wanted Gary all to herself, she didn't want the conversation to end, but the spell was broken and looking around realised that there were only two people left standing at the bar and it had gone midnight. Nick congratulated her on her audition and said they hadn't fully decided on the cast, as there were some more auditions to hold. Some teachers weren't back from the holidays yet, because their school term didn't start until the following week.

Rachel wanted him to go, she knew she ought to go home but somehow couldn't leave. Then the barman came over having packed up and said they had to go and let him lock the hall. The three of them left together and with cheery casual good nights Rachel got in the car to drive home. She'd had a few drinks and Lennie came into her mind. She made a mental note not to drink and drive again and made her way home very cautiously.

Martin wasn't in when she got home and she started to worry. The relaxed feeling she'd had all the way home dissolved as she thought of plane crashes and car accidents then spotted the note pinned to the kitchen door. In spidery scrawl Junata had written 'Sir cum tomorrow'. She felt relief and then inexplicable annoyance. Why couldn't he have called her himself earlier?

As she lay drifting off to sleep alone in the large bed, she went over the conversation with Gary. They'd discussed films and shows they'd both seen and shared feelings about people and life but did not touch on anything personal. She actually knew very little about him and she wanted to know more, no, everything. He made her feel interesting and attractive, it was a very good feeling.

Chapter 13

Wednesday afternoon Sylvia came round. Max and Lauren disappeared upstairs to play with Ben and James while Rachel and Sylvia sat on the small patio at the back with Charlotte at their feet. Sylvia looked better. She'd put on a little make-up and was chatty and lively. Rachel was relieved, dismissed her worries and started to relax.

Sylvia still chain-smoked and kept apologizing to Rachel, she said she knew she shouldn't when she was breast feeding but it was so difficult to give up. Charlotte gurgled happily, sitting on a mat in the shade with a pile of toys around her. She hadn't started crawling yet, she had no need. Sylvia seemed to carry her everywhere and with two older brothers she usually got whatever she wanted brought to her. Sylvia wasn't as edgy as before and apart from occasionally losing track of what she'd been saying (something Rachel remembered well) she chattered away.

After a while, Rachel brought up the subject of a housemaid asking Sylvia why she didn't get someone in just so that she could have a break and time to herself every so often. Sylvia bristled. She said she'd tried a few but they never quite got things right and she always felt guilty so it only made her feel worse. Anyway, if she was in the UK she'd have to cope.

'It's not a matter of coping,' said Rachel 'People cope with what they have to. If you've got the opportunity to make your life easier then you should take it. It shouldn't be something to feel guilty about, plus in the UK you'd probably have family around or at least crèche facilities everywhere.'

She spoke as gently as she could, trying not to sound like an officious health visitor but saw Sylvia tighten up and light another cigarette.

'Yeah, well I'm getting a bit sick of people telling me what I should and shouldn't do.' Her little bright eyes, glazed over.

'Hey I'm sorry. You're right, I'm always poking my nose in. Do you remember when I tried to tell you to calm down that night we went out with those ten marines. You told me I was a boring old fart and you were probably right.'

Sylvia looked vague for a minute as though she was reaching into some distance recess of her memory. Then she snapped back into life taking the opportunity to change the subject.

'Did I call you that?' she laughed. Then out of the blue she said, 'Thanks for inviting me over today, you've always been a really good friend to me Rachel.

Sorry I snapped just now. I've been a bit tired, well very tired. Don't worry about me. I'm going to be fine.' Then before Rachel could reply she said, 'Shall I make another cup of tea? I'm parched.'

When she returned, she smiled and asked Rachel if she'd gone to the auditions. Pleased that she'd remembered, Rachel gladly took the opportunity to talk about something else. She kicked herself for touching on what was obviously a sore point with Sylvia. They got back on to neutral ground, the incident was pushed aside, and Sylvia once again seemed chatty and bright.

As she was leaving, Rachel suggested they meet again the following week – maybe go to a park with all the children.

Sylvia replied 'Oh yes that would be lovely, the children would love that.' She gave Rachel a hug, thanked her and waved goodbye.

Rachel was pleased, it was good to see Sylvia more on her normal form and even the outburst had been a reminder of her old, blunt self. She'd never been one to mince her words and it was something Rachel admired about her.

Martin came back at six; he'd phoned earlier to say he had gone straight to work from the airport and would be home for dinner. Rachel reheated the casserole she'd cooked the night before and they ate with the children. It was good to sit down as a family. Martin was in a good mood; he'd had a successful trip and was chatting and joking with Max and Lauren. After dinner, he played with them, throwing them up in the air and swinging them round. They were screeching with delight calling for more. He started to tickle them.

'That's enough now,' said Rachel 'You'll get them over excited. Come on you two, get into the bath you've got school tomorrow.'

'Oh Mum!' They both moaned.

'Oh Mu-um,' joined in Martin. 'You're getting boring in your old age,' he said laughing.

'Right well you can bath them and put them to bed.' She was cross, it was the second time that day she'd heard the word boring associated with her.

'Uh oh!' said Martin, 'Come on kids, up the stairs. Last one up is a soggy banana!' They raced upstairs, Martin pretending he couldn't quite catch them up.

Max and Lauren took a long time to settle and wanted Mummy to kiss them goodnight. When she came back down to the living room she asked Martin about his trip. He told her in great detail who he'd seen and what it meant for the bank. Eventually he asked her what she'd been up to and she reminded him about the auditions. She told him how it had gone and described Mary Watson and how poor old Nick had got his work cut out directing her.

'Well let's hope you get a better part than her, then you can show the pompous old cow.'

'I don't think so,' said Rachel, 'she has got the most amazing voice.'

'So have you, and I can't see her in the role of

Nellie Forbush, can you?'

Rachel laughed; she was surprised and pleased at what was from Martin a huge compliment. She was also amazed that he knew the name of the leading lady. Perhaps he was interested, after all.

'No, but she'll be expecting it,' she said.

'I can't see Nick pandering to her prima donna attitude. When will you know?'

'Tomorrow I expect. There are more auditions tonight.'

'Shall we go out tomorrow night? See what Kathy and George are doing. We haven't been out with them for a while.'

'Okay. I'll give Kathy a ring in the morning.'

Rachel realised that she hadn't seen Martin this relaxed for a long time. It made her conscious of how distant they'd become in the last few years and she resolved to try to make things better.

Martin was particularly attentive and gentle that night and Rachel realised she couldn't remember the last time they'd made love. At first, it didn't feel quite right and she felt guilty when, 'What does he want?' popped into her head. She pushed the thought away and told herself to relax. He spent time kissing, stroking fondling, and rousing her. Her whole body, tingled and then surged with a need, all her senses concentrated on the centre of her desire. Her juices flowed and she rose towards orgasm. Her breath shortened, the lips of her womanhood throbbed with expectation but he wouldn't enter her. Her back arched as he massaged her nipples, erect and responsive. Then her pelvis thrust upwards as the spring inside her released sending spasms of pure pleasure through her whole being. She let out a moan, and...

'Mummy!'

They looked at one another and grimaced. Martin rolled off with a groan and Rachel slid out of bed. Pulling on a T-shirt, she went through to Max. He lay at the wrong end of the bed, his duvet in a pile on the floor, fast asleep. Gently she turned him back to put his head on the pillow and covered him up again. She stroked his cheek and lightly kissed him before returning to bed. Martin was snoring, lying on his back. She climbed in beside him with a sigh and prodded his side to make him turn over. The snoring ceased and she fell quickly asleep.

She was at a party, Sylvia was there, dancing on her own in the middle of the floor, smiling and laughing. Suddenly Rachel realised that Sylvia had no clothes on and she tried to tell her but Mary Watson kept standing in her way. She tried to get to Gary but Gary left with Nina and Mary was telling her she was boring. She couldn't move. Mary sat down and told her that she didn't have a part because she was too boring and then she started laughing and dancing. She tried to get up, she wanted to tell them they were wrong but no words came out. She felt a hand on her shoulder but didn't know whose it was. It was comforting, reassuring. She tried to turn her head.

She woke with a start; the room was in darkness. The feeling of panic slowly faded and she couldn't remember exactly what she'd been dreaming. The sound of the call to prayer started up from the mosque two roads away, the slightly mournful, eerie but at the same time beautiful wail pervaded the room and her head before she could sleep again.

The dream left her feeling subdued and heavy the next day. She rang Kathy from work and they arranged to go for a Mexican meal that night. Gillian Bright rang when she got home reminding her about squash. Rachel had completely forgotten, she felt guilty and arranged to meet her on Saturday evening for a game and then asked her if she and Richard would like to join them at the Mexican. She half hoped they would be busy but Gillian said they'd love to go. She phoned Kathy again to tell her. Kathy was of course delighted, the more the merrier, it was Martin she wasn't sure would be pleased. He would be looking forward to a relaxed evening with good friends, if he wasn't in a sociable mood he could be downright rude with people he hadn't met before.

Packing the children's swimming gear and thinking how to approach Martin when he came in, the phone rang again. It was Nick.

'Hello Nellie.'

'I'm sorry?'

'It's Nick here.'

'Oh hello Nick. Who did you say hello to, just then?'

'You, I want you to play Nellie Forbush.'

Silence.

'Rachel?'

'But that's the biggest part, isn't it?'

'It's the lead, yes.'

'Oh! Oh shit! Brilliant! Thank you,' she didn't know quite what to say.

'I take it that's a yes then?'

'God yes! I'm just a bit shocked, actually.'

'No doubt in my mind – first rehearsals Sunday at eight – see you then.'

'Yes. Thanks Nick, see you.'

She put down the phone, shaking. Her dream broke and she smiled thinking, 'I'll show you who's boring.'

A feeling of excitement filled her. She heard Martin's key in the door and rushed to open it. Martin nearly fell through the doorway.

'Bloody hell Rachel, what are you doing?'

'I've got the main part in South Pacific!'

'You what?'

'Me, I've got the main part, Nellie Forbush!' She was like a little kid, blushing with pleasure.

'Well done, told you, you would, didn't I? What part has Mary Watson got?'

'Oh I don't know. I forgot to ask, I was so shocked.'

'What's happening tonight?' He suddenly interrupted.

'Oh, we're meeting in The Intercon at eight,' adding quickly, 'Richard and Gillian Bright are coming as well.'

'Who are they?'

'Oh they're friends of Kathy and George. I met them at the party last week, they're good company. You're sailing this afternoon, aren't you? I'll have to go; I'll be late for the children's swimming lesson. Max! Lauren! Come on.'

The children came running downstairs. Rachel kissed Martin quickly and left, she wasn't going to give him the chance to find out that she'd invited Richard and Gillian.

Mary Watson wasn't at the pool that afternoon. Rachel was quite relieved. She was dying to share her excitement with somebody and she'd have had to play it down if Mary had been around. She sat with Sylvia and Althea. Neither asked her so she told them anyway.

Althea congratulated her and asked if she'd seen Mary.

'No, I haven't. Do you think she'll be upset?'

'Oh yes, of course she will be. Mind you, she'd have looked ridiculous in that role. It'll do her good to know that she hasn't got the monopoly on the best singing parts. Mind you, she'll probably make out that the part she has got is in fact the most important in the production.'

They laughed. Sylvia was feeding Charlotte, and she joined in when they laughed.

'Well done, Rachel. I'm really pleased for you. You'll be excellent I'm sure.' She sounded completely sincere.

'Could you not get a baby-sitter this afternoon, Sylvia?' Althea asked. Rachel winced.

'What do you mean?' Sylvia responded calmly.

'Oh it's just that last week you left Charlotte at home to bring the boys down.'

'Oh, right. No, I had to fire her, she wasn't right?' she smiled.

Althea and Rachel exchanged glances.

'I'll see you next Wednesday, with the children, Sylvia?'

'Wednesday – oh, I can't. Actually Rachel, you don't work on Saturdays, do you?' 'No I don't.'

'Do you think you could look after my three in the morning. I've got a doctor's appointment and Jim's working,' she trailed off. Ben and James went to a different school to Max and Lauren and their school week started on a Sunday.

'Yes of course, will you bring them round? Lauren and Max will be at school, of course.'

'Could you come and get them? I won't have the car.'

'Yes, sure. I'll come about nine, if that's early enough?'

'Um, yes, yes thanks,' she said smiling again. She actually seemed relaxed, almost serene.

Chapter 14

The Mexican restaurant was packed with people. The lights were low, a Filippino band played loudly at one end, the female singer doing an excellent impersonation of Madonna's voice. The level of chatter competed with the music; animated, lively groups let out occasional roars of laughter.

It was no place for a quiet, romantic meal. Rachel immediately spotted Kathy at the bar, holding court with Richard, Gillian and George listening as she told them some anecdote from her day at the office. Her hands gesticulated wildly as she talked and she was laughing unrestrainedly at her own story as Rachel and Martin came up to join them. Martin had already met Richard who had just started sailing so he was in his element being able to talk to a captive audience about the joy and exhilaration he was due if he took up the sport seriously. George, who had never tried sailing, joined them in conversation anyway and the women moved together. They had to wait for a table so they stood at the bar drinking and chatting to the numerous people they knew and waving to others who already sat at tables. Waitresses weaved across the room with trays laden with margheuritas and plates of sizzling meat and vegetables.

They eventually got to sit down and enjoyed burritos and fajitas along with more than a couple of jugs of margheurita, becoming louder and funnier as the night went on. Something made Rachel look up and across the room. Her heart and stomach seemed to lunge together as she caught sight of Gary and Nina at another table. They were with a group of ex SAS guys who now worked for the local military. Rachel had seen them at the pool. All extremely fit men, a few of them were married with kids. The wives were all stunning. She tried to concentrate on what Kathy was saying but found it difficult to restrain herself from looking over.

Kathy caught the direction of her eyes as Gary and Nina were standing up to leave and called out, 'Gary!'

Rachel felt herself trembling within while outwardly she tried to remain as cool as possible. Gary and Nina made their way over to the table smiling and friendly.

'Good to see you both' said Kathy. 'Are you going to join us for a drink?' She introduced them to Martin, Richard and Gillian and added 'And you know Rachel.'

He looked at Rachel as he said, 'Yes, of course. Well done on getting the part.'

She grinned and replied in a voice, which surprised her in its normality, 'Oh thanks very much.'

Gary looked back at Kathy, 'Would love to join

you, but I've got to take Nina and the kids to the airport early in the morning.'

'Oh, off somewhere nice?' Richard asked, unable to take his eyes off Nina in a short, tight skirt, revealing never ending tanned legs and a simple black blouse.

'I'm going home,' said Nina. 'This has been a holiday. Children have to be back in school on Monday. They had a slightly extended holiday so that Paul could have his birthday with Gary.'

'We'd better make a move,' interrupted Gary. 'Sorry we can't stay. See you later,' he said with a smile. His whole face was charming and warm as he looked at everyone around the table and briefly, oh so briefly he held Rachel's eyes causing a strange jolt in her throat and chest. Then they left.

'Wow! Who is she?' asked Richard following the elegant sway of Nina out of the restaurant.

Gillian nudged him in the ribs laughing, 'Oy! Eyes off you pervert. She was at Kathy's last week but you were too drunk to notice.'

Richard laughed and patted himself on the hand saying 'Down boy, down.' They all laughed.

That's Gary Forest, he's working as an engineer here. He's helping out with your show, isn't he Rachel?'

'Yes, he's stage manager. Seems a really nice guy.' She sounded casual, but was in fact trying to get control of her distracted sensibility.

'And Nina,' Kathy continued, 'is his ex-wife.'

Rachel looked up sharply.

'His ex?' said Martin 'What's she doing here then?'

'Wish I got on with my ex so well,' said Richard looking at Gillian knowingly.

'God, yes!' said Gillian. 'If she was out here, it would be to cut your balls off, not to enjoy a civilized meal with you.'

'They got married when she was very young, had two children and then things didn't work out, but they've remained good friends. The kids are at boarding school as she does a lot of modelling,' said Kathy who had obviously managed to find out as much as possible about them.

'That's just weird,' said Martin.

Richard said seriously, 'What do you think, Gillian? Shall I invite Sheila over for a holiday next week?'

'Over my dead body!' she retorted.

'Just jesting, just jesting.'

Everybody laughed again. Rachel tried in vain to analyse her strange reaction to the news that Gary was not married.

People were getting up to dance near the band. Kathy grabbed Martin sitting next to her and dragged him up, protesting, to join her. George looked at Rachel and said, 'Come on then, let me impress you with my athletic skills on the dance floor.' He stood up, wavering slightly, his nose redder than usual, his short, podgy figure teetering. She giggled and stood up realising that she was none too steady herself. Richard and Gillian joined them and they lost themselves in the thumping rocking beat of the music, the margheuritas freeing their inhibitions and their sense of time. Normally, so good at not drinking too much or staying out too late since the children had come along, Rachel thought, 'What the hell,' and drank and danced the night away. Staying out until four seemed like a good idea.

Staying out until four was not a good idea. Martin still managed to go sailing, Rachel could barely move. Her head was now doing the thumping and rocking. Every sound the children made jangled her nerves. She couldn't face taking them out anywhere so they fussed and bothered her in their boredom.

Martin came back around lunch time and they took the kids to Macdonald's and then to the video shop to let the children choose a couple of films.

'Never again,' she said to Martin as she fell into bed at half past eight in the evening, 'I think I'm going to die.'

Chapter 15

As Sylvia drove away from Rachel's house on Wednesday afternoon the black cloud came down once more. She'd done well at hiding it by smiling and laughing. Couldn't let anybody see, mustn't let anyone know that she was a useless mother. Rachel, so perfect, so sensible, always in control of herself, her life. It was easy for her. She never worried, always said the right thing, always had an answer. The black cloud pressed in, pushing against her brain, forcing its way towards her eyes trying to get out of her head to wrap itself around her and suffocate her. Everything around her was black, different shades of black. Must concentrate, must concentrate. Get the children home, get their tea, bath them, put them to bed. Must have Jim's dinner on the table.

Everything felt heavy, a weight dragging on her, pulling her down. She came to some traffic lights, just changing to red and felt the normal urge to put her foot down and just go on, straight on and see what happened. She saw the car colliding, crashing into a wall or a huge lorry and smashing into pieces. She slowed down and stopped, waiting for green. Can't hurt the children, must look after the children. The cloud was outside her head now. 'It must have slipped through from the back of my eyes, she thought as she felt it around her head and wrapping itself around her body.

She got the children home, did all the things she was meant to do. By seven the children were all in bed, the dinner was on, baby fed. 'Maybe she'll sleep tonight,' she said to herself as she did every night. She sat waiting for Jim to come home, staring unseeing at the wall in front of her. She wasn't really there, just this entity sitting in a black shroud on a settee looking inwards. Her insides felt as if they were draining down into a huge, dark empty pit, not her physical body but her very soul. Pouring, slowly but steadily like sand in an hourglass, away. And then it came to her, like a wave of light. Fleeting but true, the answer.

She went through the motions on Thursday, made arrangements with Rachel to look after the children on Saturday morning and a sense of calm began to settle through her. Friday went by slowly. Jim was working a weekend shift at the hospital. Everyone she knew was busy doing different family things. The boys played quite happily together, ignoring her as they were used to being ignored by her. She went through the whole flat cleaning, tidying and polishing until, satisfied, she sat down on the sofa and watched Charlotte in the playpen. She was tired, so tired.

Jim came home to find her in the kitchen finishing

off the dinner. She smiled brightly, cheerfully and asked him how he was. He smiled back, kissed her and said he was knackered. He felt relief. It had been difficult coming home the last few months. Sometimes he felt as if she wasn't even aware he was there. It had been the same when Ben was born but only for a couple of weeks. He knew he'd ignored it, hoping, sure, it would pass but it had been a long time, apart from odd phases when she was fine, usually when other people were around. As he got himself a beer and offered her one, she accepted. It had been a while since she'd sat and had a beer with him as well. He suddenly felt guilty, realising he'd really let time go by. Anyway, maybe things would go back to normal now, he thought, vowing he would try and take her out more, help with the children when he was home.

They ate dinner together and she was chatty and almost excited. She put the children to bed and they had a couple more beers and watched some TV. Charlotte had not woken. At eleven, she got up to go to bed, kissed him and gave him a brief, strong hug. He said that he would be through in a minute but cracked open another beer with a sigh and felt hopeful that the Sylvia he loved was back. He fell asleep in front of the TV and crawled quietly into bed at one o'clock. She was on her side sleeping peacefully. He set the alarm for seven and went to sleep.

When she could hear his peaceful breathing, she opened her eyes and lay for a while. Then slowly, quietly she slid out of the bed. First, she went through to the boys, pulled fallen duvets back up, kissed them softly, and stroked their heads. Then she went through to Charlotte and taking her out of the cot, put her to her breast. The baby's mouth automatically latched on, and sucked. Sylvia rocked steadily. 'Everything is going to be all right now. You'll be all right now,' she crooned. When Charlotte's head drooped back away from her, satisfied and full, Sylvia carefully placed her back in the small cot and tucked the blanket around her. She wound up the musical bear tied to the cot sides and left as the hollow, tinkle of Teddy Bear's picnic twinkled out.

In the hall, she pulled on the tracksuit she had put in the cupboard and picked up the plastic bag that she had hidden underneath some towels. Then she went into the kitchen, made up bottles of formula milk and put them in the fridge. She took a sealed envelope from the bag and placed it on the counter next to the toaster. Silently she made her way to the front door, took the car keys from the hook, and let herself out.

Getting into the car, she put the plastic bag on the seat beside her with a small clink. There were a few cars still on the roads, but nobody on the streets. It was ten past three in the morning. She drove to the waterfront and pulled into a large parking bay, stopping between two empty cars well away from a streetlight. She reached over to the plastic bag and took out the whisky and the small bottle of pills. The first mouthful burnt its way down her throat, punching her hot and hard in the gullet. She took three or four more slow mouthfuls and then opened the lid of the pills. One pill, one slug, one pill one slug. Twenty pills went down. She could feel the dragging sensation lifting. Lights flashed in her head. Everything was clear. She stepped out of the car and made her way to the steps leading down to the beach. On the sand, it was difficult to walk, but she hardly noticed. The dark, inky water lay silent and unwavering before her and beckoned. She carried straight on into the cool, welcoming embrace of the sea. The black cloud slid away and dissolved, she saw a bright whiteness and a feeling of euphoria swept through her. This was right; the children would be safe now. Everyone would be better off. This was the only right thing she'd ever done. And the black water took her in silently.

Jim's alarm went off. He switched it off, got out of bed and headed for the shower. He'd seen that Sylvia wasn't there but that was not unusual. The majority of nights she ended up sleeping in Charlotte's room. As he turned on the shower, he heard the baby cry. Stepping under the fast flowing steaming water, he blotted out any external noise. Stepping out he could hear Charlotte screaming. Desperate cries of hunger and discomfort. He wrapped a towel around his waist and went into the bedroom. He opened the bedroom door and shouted for Sylvia. There was no reply. He went in to Charlotte and picked her up. She was soaking wet. He took off her sleep suit and changed her nappy wondering where Sylvia had gone. He carried Charlotte down to the boys' room. Putting his head round the door, he saw them sitting in their pyjamas watching a video. 'Where's

Mummy?' They looked at him and shrugged, 'Don't know.'

A niggle of fear started in the pit of his stomach. He went through to the empty lounge, and into the empty kitchen. The niggle started to grow, spreading up to his chest and throat. He saw the envelope. He put Charlotte down; briefly placated by the change of nappy and a cuddle, she now started to scream again. He opened the envelope with trembling fingers. As he read, the fear became pain and his heart seemed to stop. The whole world stopped.

She told him how much she loved him and the children, that she wasn't good enough for them, that they would all be better off now. She left instructions on how to make up the baby's milk and when to give her solids. She told him that there were two bottles in the fridge but he needed to warm them first. She said that James had gym on Sunday so mustn't forget his kit and that Ben had a spelling test. She told him where the car was and that Rachel was looking after the children that morning. He felt sick and then numb. Charlotte's scream got through and he picked her up, took a bottle out of the fridge and warmed it. Then he sat in the lounge holding her, holding the bottle to her mouth. She resisted at first but hunger got the better of her and she drank greedily. He rocked steadily, dazed. He couldn't think, wasn't sure what had happened, where she'd gone. Luckily, the boys did not come through. Charlotte finished the bottle and dozed. He burped her gently, laid her in the playpen and went to the phone.

The phone rang by Rachel's ear. She had planned to get an extra hour's sleep but Martin's alarm had woken them both and as she'd had an early night she was lying there wide awake and about to get up. The phone surprised her and she picked up the receiver saying hello inquiringly.

'Rachel, its Jim, Jim Burroughs' something in his voice made her sit up.

'Hi, Jim.'

'Rachel, um Sylvia said you were looking after the children today.'

'Yes'.

'Um, it's well, it's Sylvia.'

She heard the break in his voice, 'What is it Jim? What's happened?'

'I don't know, that is, she's gone.'

'Gone?'

'Oh God I don't know, I've got a note and....'

'I'll be there. I'm coming round now.'

She put the phone down and jumped out of bed. Her heart pumped, her guts felt hollow, and all her intuition told her that something terrible had happened.

'What's going on?' said Martin when he saw her face.

'Sylvia's gone missing.'

'What do you mean, gone missing?'

'I don't know, she's left a note and she's gone. We've got to go round there.'

'I've got to get to work.'

'You're not going to bloody work; you're coming with me.'

She threw on some clothes and raced downstairs. Martin followed, stunned by her tone.

'Junata, we've got to leave now, can you get the kids' lunch boxes? ' She spoke calmly but firmly.

'We'll take separate cars – I'll drop the kids off at school and meet you at Jim's,' Rachel said.

Martin headed out and Rachel hurried the children into her car, trying to behave normally.

She was frightened, very frightened but some overriding control told her she would be of no use if she lost her head. She arrived at the flat to find Martin trying to calm down Jim and get him to tell him exactly what had happened. Jim was beside himself with anxiety, talking about where they might find her. He was not admitting to the worst. He said he had phoned the police and the hospitals but nothing so far. He told them where she'd said the car would be. Martin said they should go and find the car. Rachel said she'd take care of the children and then join them.

The two men left and Rachel gathered together nappies and changes for Charlotte. Then she went through to the boys and cheerily got them to get dressed and ready to go.

'Where's my Mum?' asked James.

'Oh she's had to go out. You're coming over to my house today, remember?'

This seemed to satisfy him. She took them to her house. Junata was delighted to have a little baby to look after, and cuddled and cooed over her.

'I have to go out again Junata. Can you manage?'

'Yes madam. There is some problem?'

'I'll explain later. Thanks Junata,' she said and turned to the boys, 'Junata will make you some breakfast, I've just got to go out, but I'll be back later.' She forced herself to smile at them.

Rachel drove to the spot described by Jim. She saw Martin's car parked next to Sylvia's. There was nobody else in sight. Getting out of the car, she went over to Sylvia's and saw the bottle, saw the pills and a gasp of horror escaped her. She ran down onto the beach and saw Martin sitting on a rock. She ran, stumbling across the heavy sand to join him, 'What's happened? Where's Jim?'

Tears were streaming down Martin's face. 'Oh God, oh God!' cried Rachel and they held each other crying.

Martin explained that they had phoned some friends of Jim. They came down and they all looked up and down the beach. Then the police came. Apparently, someone had found a body, and they took Jim to identify. John and Karen went with him and John came back to tell him. It was Sylvia. She was dead.

Jim was kept under sedation at the local hospital for a few days and the children stayed with Rachel until Jim's parents arrived. His parents got the first flight they could to look after the children, and try to explain to the boys that their mummy wouldn't be coming back. They all flew back with Sylvia's body for a funeral at home.

The whole town was affected. Something awful, traumatic had put a dint in their superficial, finely balanced well being. Everyone teetered slightly, every mother made acutely aware of their role, their feelings. Very few understood and many saw it as a selfish, wicked act. Too scared to think too deeply about what she must have been feeling, too dangerous to step too close to morbid, sinking depression, they took the easy routine of condemnation and self-congratulation that they would never do such a thing. Rachel and other friends were wracked with guilt. Maybe they could have done something, said something. If only they'd seen it coming or maybe they had seen it coming but didn't want to accept it. Rachel felt this overriding need to talk to her and the horror of knowing that she would never speak to her again left an unbearable ache in the pit of her stomach.

A memorial service was held and the church was overflowing with people. The vicar's words were an excellent tribute to the kind, loving Sylvia people remembered. A couple of friends read passages and then a lady stood up, that Rachel didn't know very well but recognised as the wife of the Club manager with a young baby the same age as Charlotte that she'd seen with Sylvia. She was rigid and trembling, her face pale and strained. In her shaking hands, she held a piece of paper but in a clear, strong voice she read.

When someone has a broken leg, we can sympathise

When someone has a broken heart, we can empathise

But when someone has a broken soul

No outward sign or loss of control

We only see the external shell

The perfect mother hiding her hell

A loving, caring friend and wife

No one could have known her terrible strife

Reflections too terrifying and too deep

An internal sickness causing that soul to weep

Our hearts go out to the loved ones left behind

But let's pray for Sylvia and her hard sought peace of mind

After the service, people milled about outside the church sombre and lost for words. To talk of ordinary things seemed inappropriate, to smile would be somehow offensive, and yet life does have to go on and there were ordinary things to be said and done and it would do no good to feel guilty about enjoying yourself. Rachel left quickly with tears streaming down her face. Martin held a protective arm around her shoulders. They drove home in silence, then Martin had to go back to work and the children needed help with their homework and then it was teatime, bath, and bed. So, life did go on, but something had shifted, slid and tremored and come to rest again. Everything looked and seemed the same but deep within a new precarious balance had been found, making an indefinable yet profound difference.

Chapter 16

The strange hollow in the bottom of her stomach remained. She tried talking to Martin about Sylvia but he did not want to think about it, analyse it or discuss it. He pushed it away and told Rachel not to dwell. Therefore, she dealt with it herself. The choral rehearsals got well under way and she found a confidence in herself that she had never had before. People complimented and encouraged her and she enjoyed the attention. Gary was at most rehearsals and she found herself looking forward to seeing him and talking to him. He was always easy, always pleased to see her and gave her little compliments here and there or teased her in a friendly, intimate way, sharing private jokes.

She became brighter, happier at home and work. Nothing seemed to annoy her, she had endless patience with the children, with the people she met and with Martin. When he complained or criticised her she laughed it off so he began to do it more. Her light and airy attitude annoyed him, and yet she was more loving, attentive, and sexual than she had been for years. It was as though Sylvia's death so terribly sad and wasteful had shaken her out of a rut and filled her with a zest and determination to enjoy life. She felt as if she was emerging from some sort of cocoon. The perfect wife and mother, working, running after the children, dinner on the table when Martin was home. She continued to do these things but the choral group was for her. She was doing something she found she was good at and, for which people praised her. It was as if she were doing it for Sylvia, who had lost sight of herself.

Jane phoned almost daily to report on the progress of her pregnancy. She had thrown herself into the role of mother to be and though there was still very little change in the shape of her body, she had a wardrobe of pretty, maternity clothes.

September slipped into October and the weather cooled to around thirty-five degrees centigrade. Jim packed up his life in the Middle East and went back to the UK to join the children. With no constant reminder, the majority of people thought no more about Sylvia or Jim and the children, and the town breathed out and carried on; the social calendar in the run up to Christmas was becoming more and more hectic.

As October sped into November, there were balls or dinner dances every weekend, dinners with friends and business partners and of course rehearsals during the week. The weather was gorgeous, warm without humidity, and time spent taking the children here and there was comfortable and easy. Rachel and Martin were both so busy that she didn't even notice the times when he was away. She even went along with her friends to dinner dances without him, if he was travelling, and had a great time. She had got to know so many new people and everyone went to the same does. Quite often Gary would be there and she'd have a dance and a chat with him. With the growth in confidence, Rachel began to look at her own appearance. She frowned in disgust at all the clothes hanging up in her wardrobe. Some of them she'd had for eight years; it was time to get a new look.

Rachel played squash with Gillian every Saturday. After the game, they would have a couple of drinks and a chat. As they became more confident in one another, their conversations moved tentatively from general subjects onto a more personal level. Rachel had learnt the hard way about the superficial social climbers; women she had really liked because they'd been so friendly and open, who had told her quite intimate details of their lives and drawn her into sharing some of her more personal feelings. They had seemed to genuinely like her and enjoy her company only to find that they dropped her the minute they realised she was not going to be useful to them socially and that her personal confidences had been discussed with numerous other 'friends' around town. She liked Gillian and was beginning to trust her as a friend.

One Saturday, they decided go up to the neighbouring city to do some early Christmas shopping. There were proper shopping malls there and a new one had opened the previous year. Rachel arranged for the children to go to a friend's house after school so that they had the whole day.

Rachel drove along the highway that took them through a small town and then there was nothing but the flat, desert reaching to the coast on the left and stretching off endlessly to the right. On the route, there were occasional buildings and a few very basic roadside cafes for truck drivers. They passed small battered lorries carrying various loads including numerous goats and one with two camels kneeling in the back of a pick up with their heads held high and looking bemused. Arabs in shining Mercedes, Maseratis and Ferraris came up behind them flashing their lights and tail-gating until Rachel moved out of their way to let them race past.

Gillian began to tell Rachel about her relationship with Richard. They had both been married when they met at the health and sports club to which they both belonged. The strong attraction between them had led very quickly to an affair and then divorce from their respective partners not without a fight, particularly from Richard's wife. He had one son and still suffered from the guilt of leaving him. Rachel was fascinated; affairs were so totally outside anything she had ever known. She couldn't contemplate how if you were married, such situations arose. After all, marriage was forever.

Gillian's pale white skin had taken on a healthy glow with a light tan. She and Richard absolutely loved life in the Middle East. She told Rachel that she was delighted with the lifestyle and how friendly, kind and welcoming everyone had been to them since they arrived. She loved her job at the kindergarten and had got to know so many people of many different nationalities through working there. She and Richard had fallen in love with the desert and had spent a few weekends camping out deep in the massive dunes looking at the brilliant sky so clear and unpolluted by light from the cities. Rachel thought fondly about the times that she and Martin had done the same and said that they must go out with them one weekend. Gillian and Richard had also taken up golf and played on a sand course which had been set up on an island. They had to go by speedboat to get there and Gillian raved about the dolphins she had seen and the Ibex that roamed freely across the island and the golf course.

They chatted continually throughout the journey, talking about each other's lives and eventually saw the landmark building of the Trade Centre in the distance. The golf club appeared on the right and they passed the only hotel for miles, before coming into the main part of the city and making their way across the creek to the shopping mall. Rachel tried to explain how much had changed since she first arrived as the whole country flourished and expanded. Out of the sand, cities of modern skyscrapers and green parks were emerging on an almost daily basis, it seemed. A tribute to modern architecture, engineering and technology, it was all due to wise and insightful leadership, and of course, money being no object. They both wondered how much more they would build in the coming years.

In the mall, they were in their element with familiar high street shops from home and a few new and original shops with a great selection for Christmas presents.

Rachel went mad buying gifts for the kids and Martin and some things to post back to her Dad.

They passed a hair salon and Rachel mentioned that she really fancied getting her hair cut short. Gillian told her to go in and see if anyone was free. Never normally impulsive, Rachel went in to ask. She fully expected them to say that they were fully booked, but the stylist said she could fit her in there and then for a cut and blow dry. Gillian said she would carry on shopping and come back in an hour and suddenly Rachel was sitting in a chair with her head back over a sink praying that this was a good idea.

Gillian returned as the stylist was finishing off the blow-dry and saw Rachel smiling at her in the mirror. The effect was quite dramatic.

'Wow!' exclaimed Gillian. 'You look amazing.'

Rachel bit her lip and asked her if she meant it. The cut really had been drastic. Her hair was short and spiky around her face, pixie style.

Gillian nodded enthusiastically, 'The bob was practical and attractive but this shorter style really accentuates your eyes and high cheekbones. I hope your director approves.'

'Oh God!' said Rachel, 'I hadn't thought about that. I suppose I'll have to wear a wig, if he doesn't!'

Next, they went shopping for themselves and Rachel bought a range of different up to date outfits. With Gillian's help, she chose them all carefully to mix and match with accessories. She realised that she hadn't shopped for herself like that since before the children were born. As well as the smart-casual garments, she spoilt herself with an expensive cocktail dress. Tiny silver sequins sewn on black crepe, thin straps and a scooped neckline. The material clung to her breasts and then fell, softly over her waist and hips, without hugging, down to a few inches above her knees. It was daring but classy. She asked Gillian if she thought that she had the legs for it.

'My God' Gillian said. 'You're not even thirty yet. If you can't wear a dress like this now, you'll never be able to do it. Now let's go and look for something that covers everything for me!'

They both laughed. Finally, Gillian persuaded her to get some make-up and, something Rachel had never done, she bought a range of expensive cosmetics.

Shopping done, they drove down to the creek and bought fresh juice from a small kiosk café. They sat sipping the delicious drinks and watching the old dhows being loaded and unloaded along the edge or sailing elegantly down the middle. They were a beautiful reminder of the city's heritage as a trading port and in direct contrast to the modern city growing up on either side of the channel.

When she got home, she felt quite exhilarated. Junata said she liked her hair and said 'Very nice madam' to each item of clothing she took out of the numerous bags. Max sniffed and carried on playing computer games but was quietly thrilled to bits with the baseball cap she'd bought him and Lauren put on the

Little Mermaid T-shirt and refused to take it off for the rest of the day and night. That kept them from wanting to know what was in all the other bags.

When Martin arrived home from another business trip the following evening, Rachel was in the kitchen finishing off their evening meal. He was in a bad mood. Huffing and chucking down his briefcase he barely said hello before disappearing upstairs to change. When he came down, he got himself a beer and went through to watch sport on the TV. Rachel put the food out on the table and called them all to sit and eat. Max and Lauren chattered throughout and Rachel made light conversation trying to draw Martin out. As soon as they'd finished, the children excused themselves, and ran off. Rachel cleared the table and stacked the dishes on the side. Martin had picked up the paper. She went over to him and put her hands around his neck, and kissed him on the cheek. He didn't respond. She asked him what was wrong, and he mumbled something about the fucking idiots at work. Then he stood up and went through to the lounge again, getting another beer on the way.

Rachel put Max and Lauren to bed and put on jeans and a new open-necked sweatshirt for rehearsal. She looked in the mirror and admired her hair, then put on some make-up, which she didn't usually bother with for rehearsals. Back downstairs, she went into Martin and announced brightly that she was off. He was watching some football and barely took his eyes off the screen as he glanced up and said, 'Right see you then.'

She hesitated and then left. Driving along, she felt a mixture of anger and guilt. She hated leaving without a kiss and a smile but felt hugely hurt that he had not even noticed her hair. She rehearsed two nights a week and more often than not Martin was away or meeting friends for a drink. It was not as if she was out night after night leaving him at home. He had been out of sorts for a few weeks and it coincided with her starting the choral production. She sensed that he resented her having this interest, which she obviously enjoyed, and it angered and hurt her that he couldn't be pleased for her.

Chapter 17

That night after rehearsal where many people had admired her hair and said how good she looked, she decided to stay behind for a drink. She sat down with Gary and a couple of Irish girls in the chorus: teachers at a local primary school. They chatted and joked. Nick came over to join them and running his fingers agitatedly through what little hair he had, he sat down with a huge sigh.

'Need a drink?' asked Gary.

'Yes, a double brandy! No, just get me a pint, cheers,' Nick frowned.

Gary got up to go to the bar as Mary Watson flounced past clutching her script and heading for the door. Rachel called out bye and Mary turned with a huge smile, and called 'bye' resonantly falsely and carried on out of the door. Rachel and the teachers giggled and Nick gave a wry grin. 'Fucking bitch' he said. Gary returned and handed him the beer saying

'Having a hard time Nick?'

'No, no, everything's running very smoothly.' He raised his eyes to the ceiling and they all laughed.

The production was at that stage when everything seems to fall apart. Lines not learnt, musicians not turning up, people forgetting stage directions, everyone demanding attention for their particular role and only two weeks to the show. Somebody said, 'It'll be all right on the night.' The old adage that everybody clings to throughout amateur productions. They all discussed Mary Watson and her prima donna attitude. She had the part of Bloody Mary and as Althea Richter had predicted, it was, in her eyes, the most important role. She demanded attention constantly, every so often throwing small tantrums with Nick or the musical director.

The teachers left to go to a night club. They were on half term at their school and were off to party the night away. Rachel was left with Nick and Gary. It reminded Rachel of the first time she'd met Gary and the effect he'd had on her. That seemed such a long time ago. He still had an effect on her; her heart gave a little leap whenever she saw him and whenever they touched, which was quite often now as he often gave her a quick hug, she felt the electric shock run through her body. She never analysed it, just enjoyed it and enjoyed the friendship they'd developed. Nick was called away by someone else demanding his attention. Gary offered her another drink and still feeling anger towards Martin, she accepted. It wasn't late and she was always buzzing after rehearsing.

When Gary returned with the drinks she asked him how Nina and the kids were doing. It was strange, but it was the first time she'd mentioned Nina. They talked a great deal during and after rehearsals but about general subjects, never anything personal. From this initial, innocent question, he began telling her about his marriage and his life.

He'd graduated from university and had been totally disillusioned by the unemployment and the general mood of depression around him. He joined the army for something to do. Probably the wrong reason, but he was an active person. At school and university he had excelled in sport and couldn't stand the inactivity of being on the dole; day after day writing off for jobs and sitting waiting for the inevitable 'thank you but no thank you', so he signed up.

He excelled in the army too, loving the physical training and the discipline. He was model officer material. He was in Northern Ireland when he was 'approached.' He was asked if he would like to try for Special Forces and joined a group of twenty other hopefuls in Wales.

It was the start of a rigorous training and selection procedure, which many men did not make. He passed and suddenly he was a member of the elite SAS. Rachel was fascinated and amazed. She had heard people mention that Gary was ex-SAS and since the Gulf War, it was not unusual to meet men who had been or still were involved with the military. There was a constant military presence and a number had left the forces and made use of contacts made during the war to find work in the region. Gary met Nina when he was on leave. She was twenty-one, beautiful, lively and independent. She worked as a model and was reasonably successful; doing magazine work and TV commercials, she didn't seem to mind his erratic work. In fact, his absence for sometimes months at a time seemed to make the relationship all the more exciting and romantic. She coped well with the necessary secrecy about his job and not knowing where he was or when she might see him next. They got married nine months after they first met and she moved to his base town, confident that she would be able to get work and make new friends. Then she discovered that she was pregnant. They were both delighted but it changed everything. She could no longer work apart from a few maternity shoots and when the baby arrived, she found herself alone most of the time with this large responsibility and she became paranoid about something happening to Gary. She did have friends but she resented him not being there. When he came home all she could do was cry. She hated herself for being that way and that made the crying worse. He did what he could to reassure her and then the Falklands war broke out.

He was on South Georgia. He had received orders to attack at first light. It was cold, so very cold but they were all accustomed to discomfort. A few of the lads made jokes but as they all caught snatches of sleep between watches, the tension mounted. They were in the front line. They were going to die. The feeling was so strong, so definite, unlike any other mission he'd been involved in where you thrived on adrenalin, on the edge, close to death at any moment but with an underlying confidence that if you did the job right you would survive. This was different, the odds were against them. There might be eventual victory but their lives would be the price. Like drowning, he thought about his whole life, about the point of it all and God he wanted to be with Nina and Paul. All the petty, silly rows, all the situations he'd been in where he'd got angry or upset. All seemed so pointless so trivial. He vowed to himself that if he did survive, he'd never be annoyed by anything trivial ever again. He vowed to be a better husband, father, son. The icy wind bit into his face and he looked up at the clear sky and found the moon. Always there, somewhere, wherever he went in the world, his point of focus, his contact with Nina.

One hour to go, no one was sleeping. They all checked and rechecked their weapons, their ammunition. The knot of fear tightened in their bellies, moving up to their throats and sticking. Gary could feel his heart, hear his heart, as the fear gripped across his chest. The man on the radio, Jez, sat listening, waiting and then they heard him asking, 'Repeat, repeat,' and they watched and waited and listened as he turned to face them all. They couldn't read the expression in his eyes. He slipped off his headphones and said quietly, 'They've surrendered.' Then louder, 'They've fucking surrendered!'

Rachel was entranced. This was so far beyond her experience. Even though she'd been through the Gulf war, it had still seemed removed. Yes, she'd heard about death and destruction, she had been in England watching the news throughout the Falklands but it had all been so distant, slightly unreal. She could think how terrible it all was, but had never really considered any true involvement.

'The funny thing is,' continued Gary, 'that for all those thoughts I had, and I can still remember how I felt, not long after I got back, I was waiting for a bus and it was late and I got really angry and pissed off standing there. I was with this little old lady, who was moaning and complaining about the service and how you couldn't rely on anything. And I was there agreeing with her.'

On leave after the Falklands, their daughter was conceived. They went through a good patch when Nina had been so relieved to have him back, alive and well. But then he had to go off again, the pregnancy went by and then she had two small children. Jody was a terrible baby, she seemed to cry all day. Nina suffered badly and her mother came to stay. When Gary came home on leave it seemed that the mother-in-law had taken over but he needed attention too. The rows became nastier, more frequent. He went away again and when he returned Nina had gone back to her parents' house with the children. He had been furious, hurt and relieved. Returning had started to become worse than leaving. They remained separated, tried to make it work a couple of times but Gary was never there long enough and the recriminations would start again. They loved each other but it wasn't making them happy so they divorced. Nina got back into modelling and started travelling in the week. Her parents were quite old and unable to look after the boisterous children full time, so they went to weekly boarding school. Gary visited when he was in the country and gradually he and Nina became friends.

During the Gulf War he was involved in organising some risky operations and he realised he was starting to question what he was doing and why. He couldn't quite justify what he was doing and knew it was time to get out and move on. He dealt with a number of Arabs and made some useful contacts. His training and knowledge of structural engineering and design had proved very useful in the forces so he had not missed out on experience. His first job took him to Brunei and then he had been offered a job with a very important local man involved with the building of palaces and some impressive high-rise apartment blocks. It was proving to be very challenging but lucrative.

'But what about Nina, now?' asked Rachel. 'If you're working here, normal hours, couldn't you get back together?'

'No, too much has happened. Nina's happy. She's got a boyfriend. I've had a few relationships - you can't go back. We're very close friends and that's lucky. It works well.' He looked at Rachel and said 'What about you? Are you happy?'

'Yes, I am.' She thought for a second, 'I've got a good life.'

She looked at him and smiled. Then she looked at her watch and said, 'Shit it's half-past one!'

They looked around the room. A couple of backstage lads were still there, very drunk and putting the world to rights with Bill who was manager on duty. Everyone else had gone and they hadn't even noticed.

'God, I'd better go home.'

'Yes, you're a terrible woman keeping me talking.'

They looked at each other and laughed. Gary walked with her to the car and kissed her on the check. As she was getting in, he said, 'You make me happy.'

She felt a warm tingle spread through her. She smiled and said, 'Thank you, see you soon.'

As she drove away, she felt completely light headed and her stomach was doing strange somersaults. Over and over in her head she kept hearing him say 'You make me happy,' and each time it sent a wave of elation sweeping over her. It had to be the most beautiful thing anybody could say. It didn't ask for anything in return, it was a simple statement but perhaps the best compliment anyone could pay. She enjoyed the feeling and yet still did not move forward into admitting anything beyond friendship and mutual attraction, however exciting that attraction might be. Maybe it was naivety or maybe a denial in her, which did not allow for anything outside the marriage. She knew she thought about Gary maybe more than she ought but he was a separate entity. Her thoughts never came close to a comparison with Martin or even made her question her love for her husband. It was pure ego boost.

Chapter 18

The following day, Martin was leaving on a business trip to Jordan. Rachel had laid out clean shirts, socks, pants and ties. She was trying to get Max and Lauren dressed and sorted out for school. Martin shouted for her from their bedroom. She went through to find him holding up a pair of socks.

'For Christ's sake Rachel these have got holes in them. Can't you get anything right. Just once!' he yelled.

Rachel closed the bedroom door. She hated the children hearing shouting and arguing. Normally, she would have gone to get another pair of socks and ignored the comments but something snapped. Maybe it was that she had still been feeling good about the night before, maybe it was just the last straw after constant moods, nasty comments, and digs which up until now she'd ignored. She stopped on her way to the sock drawer and spoke in low, furious tones.

'I am sick to death of being treated like some piece of shit you just stepped in. Stop acting like a fucking baby and get your own bloody socks. You're the one who's going away. I'm the one left to run around after the children, do the shopping and most of the cooking and I work. Yes, you work hard, yes, you earn the most money to let us live the way we do. But, don't take me for granted. It's about time you showed some appreciation for what I do.'

'Oh and what is it you do? You've got a maid, you play squash and you go off rehearsing for some pathetic amateur show that makes you think you're some kind of star. It's about time you remembered who you are.'

Tears of frustration, pain and anger welled up in Rachel's eyes. She left the room and rushed into the other bathroom, the tears falling, streaming down her face. Holding on to the edge of the sink, she looked at herself in the mirror and took a deep breath. Her eyes were already red and beginning to swell. She was annoyed with herself for crying and with a huge sigh she ran the tap and splashed her face with the lukewarm water. No time to cry. Patting her eyes with a towel, she left the bathroom and went downstairs to make sure the children were having their breakfast.

Martin came down five minutes later with his suitcase and called out 'Bye'. Max and Lauren called back, 'Bye Daddy,' and carried on munching their toast.

Rachel hesitated and then went out to the hall and said, 'Don't I get a kiss then?'

'Not sure I want to,' he said.

'I'm sorry I lost my temper,' she said and reached

up to put her arms around his neck and kissed him.

He kissed her back and said, 'Yes, you should be. All this play stuff is going to your head.'

Her heart sank and she could feel a bubble of anger expanding in her chest but she held it back, she didn't want him to go away on an argument. In a quiet voice she said, 'Don't knock me for finding something I enjoy. You should be pleased I've got interests I'm good at.'

'Yes, dear,' he said condescendingly. 'Right I'd better get off. I'll ring you when I get to the hotel.'

'Okay, bye. Safe journey.'

She forced herself to smile and waved him off. Inside she burned with fury. She put on her make-up, got the children and they all left the house. In the car, she answered Lauren's insistent questions, and dropped them both off with the usual huge hug, kiss and smile and then drove to work.

Coming to the top of a fly-over she looked towards the city; towering skyscrapers and large cranes signifying more building stood in the shimmering haze beneath a pure blue sky that had only just become clear and natural after the grey residue of the Gulf War had finally dispersed. She sighed; she did love the place. The never ending warmth and sunshine, the interesting quirks of the different nationalities, the constant social life, availability of sport and drama and working hours that gave her time to do plenty of things with the children and a live-in housemaid to baby-sit and keep the house. Why then, the feeling of creeping dissatisfaction? Why, the sense of frustration and loss of identity? She arrived outside the office and realised to her horror that she couldn't actually remember driving. She had got there as though in automatic, her mind completely on other things. A dangerous thing to do with the way taxi drivers and the average motorist drove in town.

Once in the office, there was plenty to do and she pulled herself together and threw herself into her normal efficient routine. She was meeting Jane and another nurse for lunch and decided to ask Junata to pick up the children from school. She felt slightly guilty doing that but convinced herself that by going for lunch earlier she would get back in time to take them to the Club for a couple of hours.

They decided to have a pub lunch and met in one of the hotels for a bar snack. Once inside you could have been in any pub in the UK. Mock oak beams created a country look; there were small wooden tables, a mock fireplace, and a bookcase. Carlsberg, Heineken, and John Smith artefacts adorned the walls and bar. Small clusters of men in suits and ties gathered at the bar or around the tables, obviously conducting important business deals as yet another pint was downed. At the far end, a few younger men in jeans and T-shirts looking scruffy and unkempt played darts or pool. Most likely, off one of the islands or rigs for a few days leave, they looked rough and leery.

There were only two other women in there when

Rachel arrived with Jane and her friend Diedre, dark skinned women who sat separately at the bar, sipping long drinks and trying to gain eye contact with the men. It had a dark, dingy atmosphere; the smell of stale beer and tobacco hung in the air. As they sat down, and ordered some drinks and looked at the menu, more people began to arrive from work. The bar began to fill and soon a gentle, cheery hubbub knocked about the room; fresh beer, tobacco and hot food smells replaced the old ones and a genial, cosy atmosphere pervaded.

They all relaxed and chatted. Diedre was a fast-talking, lively Irish girl. She had just broken up with the latest in a string of boyfriends and was vociferously slagging off all men in an explicit, hilarious dialect. It seemed that Peter was no longer the knight in shining armour as Jane joined in the general denunciation of the male gender and Rachel found herself adding Martin to the list of selfish, arrogant, thoughtless men they knew. Each woman fed off the other, nodding excitedly and laughing gleefully when one said something that the other recognised and sympathised with precisely. Then it began to get more serious and as they talked, ate, and drank they wound each other up until quite angry, bitter things were said.

Rachel had been in these situations before and normally hated them, but now she found herself almost vitriolic in her feelings about Martin. She continued to drink and talk. A couple of men Jane knew from the rugby club came over and offered them all a drink. They pulled up chairs and one of them, Roy, a good-looking man with short cropped brown hair, small angular nose and a strong chin started the conversation with 'You girlies sneaking out behind your husbands back eh?'

Rachel groaned inwardly. Jane said they didn't actually need written permission to go out and Diedre added 'Not all of us are married.'

Rachel saw her look directly at him as she spoke, the sparkle in her eyes as she sat up straighter and leaned slightly towards him. They started to flirt and Jane and Rachel were left with the other man, Alan who began to bore them with a description of the birth of his son from his first marriage. He got to his third marriage and Rachel and Jane began to have fun winding him up. A few more people arrived and joined the jolly crowd. Jane, not drinking, said she had to go, fully expecting Rachel to do the same but Rachel decided to stay. She was having fun and getting a lot of attention, while Diedre, who seemed to have forgotten her earlier feelings about men, was laughing merrily at everything Roy said, throwing her head back and touching his arm as he continued, obviously enjoying the sound of his own voice.

Afternoon slipped into evening and Rachel did something she had never even considered before. She rang Junata and told her she would not be home until later. She spoke to the children, bribed them with promises of treats, returned to the bar to play darts and accepted the offer of another glass of wine.

As the evening went by, the bar became a heaving, jumping mass of bodies. Dancing started and Rachel danced without a care in the world and drank a few more glasses of wine. She felt free and attractive, and full of confidence. At one in the morning, her eyes began to swim and she realised she had to go. Various men tried to persuade her to stay but just holding onto her sensibilities, she staggered outside, clambered into one of the ubiquitous gold and white taxis and went home.

She felt guilty about leaving the children for the whole day but persuaded herself that she didn't do it very often so it wouldn't hurt them. She was aware that part of the guilt came from the argument she'd had with Martin. Then she felt bad about things she'd said in the pub. By the time she got home, she felt quite sober and sat in the lounge with a coffee feeling thoroughly depressed and confused. She thought about Martin and felt cross. Cross that she was always the one who made the gesture to make-up; hurt that he put down her enjoyment in the choral group and depressed about the conversation in the pub that pointed to a general condition.

If all men were the same, then was this the best she could hope for in her life? This was marriage, a slotting of two people into particular roles that you fulfilled in order to maintain an even keel. If one of you moved out of that order, then the whole boat would be rocked and unless necessary shifting of balance took place, it would capsize. She knew that she was the one shifting, knew that she had been performing dutifully and had fitted into the pattern to keep things steady. She thought back to the first year of marriage, the great times they'd had, laughing, partying, in love. Then it dawned on her; it was his refusal to shift that was rocking the boat.

She had compromised her career ambitions to follow him to the Middle East for his job; she had coped with raising a family while he worked away from home a lot. She knew he hadn't coped well with the changes children bring, even though he loved them to bits. Her weight gain, her lack of interest in sex when they were small had caused problems and now as she thought about it, they rarely had sex at all. It seemed the time had slipped by without realising the changes. They were little more than housemates sharing the same living space and children, though he spent very little time with them or her. Now all she was doing was enjoying a new interest. It had suited him that she could go out with Kathy and George or to play sport while he was away, but suddenly she was involved with something he knew nothing about. Instead of encouraging her and paying an interest in her, he was trying to squash her back into a neat little pigeonhole, and she no longer fitted.

That night she dreamed she was standing on a bridge looking down into the clear water. She was thinking of jumping and then thought 'How silly, I can swim.' She turned and saw Nick on the other side and she walked on across the bridge towards him.

Chapter 19

The next rehearsal was fraught with tension. The wardrobe lady, Libby was rushing around trying to get people to try on half made costumes between scenes. The construction team was finishing off painting scenery behind the actors. Nick was pulling his precious hair out as he got people to go over pieces again and again, reminding them all exasperatedly that the dress rehearsal was next week. Predictably, Mary threw a fit about the disturbance in the hall and how could she be expected to perform under such conditions! By the end of the night, everyone was thoroughly depressed and convinced it was going to be a disaster. Nick managed to pull everyone together with a funny and encouraging talk before telling all of them to piss off and have a good week.

Rachel bought Nick a drink and they sat, and talked for a while. Gary was still up on stage working out scene changes and checking flats. They had to use portable flats because the drama society had the stage for their annual pantomime two weeks after their show and were well under way with their own sets. Gary had devised their scenery very simply but effectively to fit inside the panto set without disturbing anything. They were already taking up valuable rehearsal time in the hall and the choral group didn't want to tread on any toes. Rachel told Nick she was starting to get really nervous but thanked him for being such a good director. He was really pleased and said that that was the first positive thing he'd heard all night. He looked worn out and sighed. 'Never again,' he said shaking his head ruefully. 'Definitely, never again.'

Rachel stood up to leave and patted his shoulder. 'It's going to be great, you'll see.' She called out bye to Gary and he came over.

'Not going already are you?' he asked.

Rachel wanted to stay but forced herself to say, 'Yes, I'm whacked and we've got a late night tomorrow.'

'Oh, what's that?'

'It's the Sailing Club Christmas party.'

'At the Hilton?'

'Yes'

'Oh right, I'll see you there. I was invited last week.'

'Oh really? It'll be interesting to see you all dressed up in your best bib and tucker. I've only ever seen you in a scruffy t-shirt and shorts.'

"I haven't got a clue what to wear,' he said with a

grin. She laughed and then had another thought, 'Oh, actually I might see you in the afternoon. I'm bringing Lauren and Max down for their swimming lessons and said I'd help with some painting.'

'Oh right, maybe – I might be working.'

'Whatever, see you tomorrow at some point.'

Again, that light feeling. On her way out, she stopped to talk to some of the girls in the chorus and quipped with a couple of the guys as they made mock leery remarks about the shorts she would be wearing on stage. She revelled in the attention she was getting and sang all the way home.

The next day, Martin arrived back from Jordan. He was in a great mood and had bought presents for all of them. As Rachel opened the bottle of perfume, he gave her a hug. She smiled and kissed him, feeling guilty for all the horrible thoughts she'd had about him.

'Right' he said, 'I've got to get changed. I'm sailing in an hour.'

'Okay. I'll be at the Club, all our rehearsals will be there now and they need a hand with painting.'

'They must be desperate if they need you to paint,' laughed Martin.

She laughed and said, 'It's all right. I've told them to give me a small brush and a large space to cover.'

Martin went up to change and rushed out again while Rachel got the children together and took them to their swimming lesson. There was a cool breeze blowing and with the temperature dropping slightly you could tell winter was coming. It was coming to the end of November and by five, few people were swimming or even in swimming costumes as the temperature fell to around twenty-five degrees centigrade. Rachel had a cup of tea with Althea and Mary. Mary talked non-stop about the show and what an organisational disaster it all was until Rachel interrupted her and said she thought it was going very well, and that Nick was doing a great job. Mary was dumb-struck for a second and then said, 'Yes well some people seem to get on better with the director than others.'

Rachel laughed and said pointedly, 'Yes they do.'

Althea quickly interrupted with, 'Well, I'm really looking forward to seeing it. I bet it's going to be good, it's just at that stage when nothing seems right. It's the same every time.'

Max and Lauren came out of the water shivering so Rachel got them quickly dressed and ready to go and paint.

'I'm just off to help with the scenery. Are you helping at all Mary?'

'No, that's not really my department,' she replied.

'Well, see you all soon.'

As soon as she was out of earshot, Mary turned to Althea. 'I tell you what, give someone a good part and it goes straight to their heads. She's completely changed since she started.'

'Looks very good on it, though,' said Althea.

'Yes, I suppose so, but you know why. You should see her with Nick and the only reason she's going painting is because Gary is the stage manager.'

'Gary?'

'Yes, very attractive, gets on well with all the girls. Apparently, he's been with all the girls in the chorus. Good looking and uses it. But is particularly friendly with Rachel.'

'Oh well I'm sure there's nothing in it. She's far too straight and she and Martin are really together.'

'Yes, I'm sure you're right,' replied Mary with a smug little shake of her head.

Althea was irritated. Mary Watson was part of a group of people who had been around forever and spent their lives watching and spreading rumours that sometimes had an unfortunate habit of proving true. And Rachel had begun to change.

Rachel had on a pair of old jeans and a T-shirt. She put old shirts on the children and went backstage to see what they could do. There were three or four of the crew and a few girls from the chorus putting finishing touches to the Bali Hi scenery. There was no sign of Gary and she felt a snatch of disappointment. She volunteered to paint one of the model palm trees and with the children's dubious help got down to work. Lauren lost interest after painting most of her hands and face so she and Max decided to entertain themselves running across the stage and jumping down. Rachel found herself spending as much time trying to control them as painting, but nobody was too worried. There was a good humoured sense of people working together, odd jokes were made and comments thrown. It was relaxed and productive.

Just before six Rachel realised she'd better get the children home and herself ready for the dance that night. She cleaned her brush and calling goodbye to the others, opened the side stage door that led to the car park. Gary was just coming towards her. He gave her a huge smile and called hello to Max and Lauren who smiled shyly at him.

As he got closer, he burst out laughing. She frowned and asked, 'What's so funny?'

'Look at your mummy kids, didn't you want to tell her? You've got paint on your nose,' he said as he reached her, 'and just about everywhere else.'

Max and Lauren giggled and Max said, 'Well she hasn't got as much on her as me and Lauren.'

'Very true, you all look as though you've been doing a very good job!' He reached out and gently rubbed at a spot of paint on Rachel's nose, 'No, you'll just have to bathe in turps when you get home.'

'Umm my favourite. Some of us have been working like Trojans in there.'

'I got held up at one of the palaces. Just going to do a bit now.'

'I've got to get Max and Lauren some tea. I'll see you tonight.'

'Okay, see you later. Bye Max, bye Lauren,' he called as they walked away.

Chapter 20

When they got home, Martin was not yet there. The children had their tea and then went to watch TV while Rachel had a bath. It was nearly time for them to go to the dance and Martin had still not come back so Rachel got the children to bed and finished getting herself ready.

She put on her new sparkly dress and carefully applied her make-up. Just as she was beginning to get quite worried, she heard Martin's key in the door. He came into the bedroom, crept up sheepishly behind where she was sitting in front of the dressing table and gave her a kiss on the cheek. She could smell the beer on his breath.

'Sorry I'm late. We won the race so I just stayed for a couple of beers afterwards.'

'Bloody hell, Martin! We're meant to be there in twenty minutes.'

She turned to face him, 'Oh! You're covered in sand.'

'All right, all right. I won't take long to get ready. Is my DJ there and can you get my shirt and bow tie while I'm in the shower?'

As he talked, he moved into the bathroom and turned on the taps. Next, she could hear him singing loudly to himself. It crossed her mind that she hadn't heard him do that for a long time. Must have been a good race. She finished her face and admired herself in the full-length mirror on the wardrobe door. She knew she looked good. Then she got out Martin's clothes and called to him that she was going downstairs. She made herself a gin and tonic and sat up at the bar in their dining area. As promised, Martin didn't take long and she heard him calling her as he came downstairs.

'Just do up these cuff links for me, can you?'

She went over and did up his cuff links, then without looking at her, he picked up the car keys and said, 'Right, are we ready?'

Rachel was crestfallen. He hadn't even noticed the dress or the extra careful touches of make-up but she wrapped up the feeling and tucked it away. She said goodbye to Junata and followed Martin out to the car.

On the way, he told her about the race in fine detail, he was lively and happy. The couple of beers seemed to have set him up for a good night out.

If Martin didn't notice how good Rachel looked, just about everyone else did. They walked onto the pool deck for reception drinks, the turquoise water shimmering bright and the underwater lights reflecting up onto the faces of those standing near to the edge. Fairy lights adorned the surrounding walls, the men looking uniformly smart in DJ's with women in an array of evening dresses; expensive ball gowns and tailor made dresses in a variety of styles and lengths chatted politely.

There was an air of opulence and sophistication as gold and diamonds glittered under the lights. But there was also a feeling of nervous restraint. Many of the women looked tense and slightly uncomfortable in their dresses and continually touched their carefully styled hair, fiddled with straps and bodices and glanced around to see what everyone else was wearing.

The majority wore black, always a safe choice, but had not taken that reserve as far as the design was concerned. Fat ladies squeezed into tight sleeveless dresses revealing flabby arms and potbellies. A couple of younger ladies with admirable cleavages had decided to wear dresses which just reached over their bottoms thus detracting from their best point and accentuating over large, dimpled thighs. Janet Bright had dared (unadvisedly) to go for a long, lime-green floaty affair. It was fussy and frilly around the shoulders and then clung to her stomach and short legs, stopping at her ankles to reveal gold T-bar shoes. With her bleached hair and green eye shadow, she looked as if she had been too close to Chernobyl at the time of the explosion. Eleanor Stevens looked fabulous in a long black dress with thin cross-back straps and a slit up one side. She wore long black gloves and a velvet choker on her slim neck.

As people arrived, they looked slightly desperate as they tried to find people they knew and moved quickly to merge into small groups and become less conspicuous. Everyone admired everyone else with over enthusiastic exclamations but gradually as the waiters replenished glasses the tension began to fade.

Rachel and Martin joined Richard and Gillian, and Kathy and George. Gillian immediately greeted Rachel by telling her how lovely she looked and Richard readily agreed looking her up and down and promising her a dance later on. They fell into chatting about what they'd all been up to and Rachel gave them an amusing description of rehearsals with Nick near combustion point and Mary Watson throwing a wobbly. As she talked and listened, she found herself looking around for Gary. She finally picked him out with a dark skinned, dark haired young nurse who was in the chorus. They were with two or three other nurses and Gary was saying something to make them all laugh. She felt a strange stab of jealousy, which caught her by surprise and she forced herself to pay attention to what Kathy was saying.

They all went through to sit down to a five-course dinner. Various people made disparaging comments all the way through and Rachel wondered how many of them ate food like that in their home country, let alone in a Hilton hotel. The wine flowed and the conversation varied from a vague attempt at discussing politics, which no one really knew enough about apart from to say how awful it all was, to the disgusting price of vegetables in the supermarket and how difficult it was to get a decent housemaid.

As the waiters served coffee, an interminable number of speeches and trophy awarding took place that was of little interest to anyone but the winners. Martin won something with his crew, Tina. He swayed up and across to the Club Chairman to receive a plaque giving Tina a hug and kiss on the cheek for the camera before returning to the table beaming. Everyone at the table clapped and cheered. Rachel gave him a kiss and congratulated him but there had been something strange about the hug and kiss with Tina, which she couldn't quite put a finger on but quickly forgot about.

The speeches were followed by a raffle with the top prize of an air ticket to London. Happy winners accepted prizes of gold jewellery, video cameras, nights in hotels and numerous dinners. A highly excitable and drunken nurse screeched and yelled when she went up to collect the air ticket, her large body and braless breasts shimmered and shook under the shiny, clinging material of her dress and the DJ called out over his microphone, 'Someone save those puppies,' as she approached the front. Everybody laughed but she didn't notice in her joy at winning the coveted prize.

Finally, the music started and a mixture of songs from the sixties, seventies, eighties and early nineties filled the room. People got up to dance immediately and before long any remnant of quiet sophistication was lost as jackets came off, ties were loosened, high heels discarded and people became hot, sweaty and intoxicated.

Martin moved towards the bar to join a throng of non-dancing males and Rachel, Gillian and Kathy went on to the dance floor. Various men asked Rachel to dance throughout the night. She was flattered and enjoyed the impact her appearance had made. Sitting down to have a drink after five or six dances she looked around for Gary and couldn't see him, then someone touched her arm and she turned to see Nick smiling down at her.

'I was going to ask you for a dance but you seem to have had more than a fair share of offers.'

'No, I'm always available for you. Come on.'

She danced with Nick to two or three lively records. He was excellent fun and moved well. She returned to the table out of breath and laughing just as Gary came over, pulled up a chair and said, 'Any chance of fitting me in for a dance, madam?'

'Oh I might be able to, I'll have to check my dance card though,' she laughed.

He sat down next to her saying hello to Richard and Gillian who had also just come off the dance floor for a rest. The four of them tried to talk but it was difficult shouting over the music and it fell to just Rachel and Gary.

'Well you look a bit different to the last time I saw you,' he said. 'I see you managed to remove all the paintwork.'

'Used a whole bottle of white spirit, actually. I'm just praying nobody lights a cigarette too close to me. You brush up well,' she said, admiring him in his DJ.

He shrugged and said, 'This old thing?' and they both laughed. 'Thanks for your help this afternoon,' he added.

'I didn't really do that much but I did enjoy it.' She paused, 'How much more is there to do?'

'Well, I left some of them there still painting so hopefully if a few people come tomorrow we should be finished before the show ends.'

They talked for a while longer and then got up to dance. Rachel felt so comfortable with him and he obviously loved to dance. At the end of the record, he took her back to the table and said he'd see her later. Rachel sipped her drink and looked around the room. Martin was still up at the bar deep in meaningful conversation and then she caught sight of Althea Richter watching her. She waved and went over to talk to her.

'Who was that gorgeous man you were just dancing with?' asked Althea.

'Who? Gary?'

'Oh that's Gary is it?'

'Why, what have you heard about him?'

'Nothing, someone mentioned a Gary that was stage manager for your show and I didn't know who it was.'

'Yes, that's Gary. He's great company, very easy going which is great for all the nervous wrecks up on stage.' Rachel kept cool, she knew that Althea was fishing and found it quite amusing.

'I hear he's quite a ladies' man.'

'Really? Where did you hear that?' Rachel's heart beat a little faster.

'Can't remember who said it, but apparently he's been with quite a few of the young single girls.' Althea seemed to emphasise the word single and Rachel began to feel oddly uncomfortable.

'Oh well, good for him!' Rachel smiled broadly at Althea and said, 'Oh I love this record – do you want to dance?'

'Yes, come on then,' agreed Althea, her intuition detecting Rachel's discomfort.

The two of them went up to dance. Althea, large and rolling, had terrific rhythm and they joined in step as Bruce Springsteen belted out. Kathy and George joined them half way through and they all tried to follow some vague dance steps but failed and ended up giggling their way back to the table.

Rachel caught the eye of Tina, who gave her a stunning smile and a little wave. Rachel smiled and waved back, mouthing 'well done' to her across the dance floor. She watched Tina swinging her hips provocatively to the golden oldie 'You keep Me Hanging On' by the Supremes; with her smooth, flat stomach and pert breasts, she looked fit and attractive. Rachel noticed that Tina's eyes flitted continually back to some point across the room. As Rachel carefully followed the gaze she saw it was aimed at the group of men around the bar including Martin. The music faded into the next song and Rachel went up to the bar to order a round and to see how Martin was doing. He was very drunk and slurring his words along with the other men with whom he was talking. It was doubtful whether any of them understood what anyone else was saying. As she came up, he put his arm round her shoulder and said to Gordon Jones 'Have you met my wife?'

'Yes we have met before,' replied Gordon looking Rachel up and down and letting his eyes linger on her cleavage, 'And may I say how ravishing your wife looks.'

'The wife does have a name,' said Rachel, 'and she can speak.'

'More's the pity,' replied Gordon, and to her disgust he and Martin laughed.

She went up to the bar and ordered a round and then on her way back, she deliberately jolted Gordon's arm so that his pint of beer sloshed all over him.

'Oh, I'm so terribly sorry,' said Rachel and walked on before he could react. When she got back to the table, she was shaking but felt secretly pleased with herself. She knew that a year ago, even six months, she would never have dared to say what she said, let alone deliberately knock beer over someone. She told Kathy what had happened and she said, 'Good for you. That Gordon Jones is a chauvinistic arsehole.'

'I'm more angry with Martin.'

'Oh Martin's too drunk to know what's going on.'

'That's no excuse.'

'Just forget it. Come on we're having a good time. Cheers!' Kathy held up her glass and Rachel held up hers. 'To hell with him' she thought and got up to dance with George. Rachel enjoyed herself immensely. She dismissed the Gordon Jones incident and threw herself into dancing. She had no shortage of men asking her to dance and received compliments from both men and women.

The number of people began to thin out and slow numbers started to play. Martin had returned to the table and Kathy was talking away to him but his eyes kept rolling back into his head as his eyelids drooped and he looked as if he would fall asleep at any moment; it was a common occurrence when he drank too much. Around the room, there were three or four men in the same state, lolling back in their chairs unable to focus on anything. Other people sat and chatted, obviously putting the world to rights at half empty tables covered in empty bottles, cigarette ash, half-filled glasses, slices of lemon, and screwed up napkins.

Judy Tzuke's 'Stay with me till Dawn' came on and Rachel unconsciously looked for Gary and found him looking for her. They moved forward onto the dance floor and his arm went around her waist. He held her hand and they swayed in time to the soft, sweet song, their bodies not quite touching. She was conscious of his hand gently on her back, of the slightly sweaty joining of the other hand in hers. Her face close to his shoulder, she could smell his skin, her other hand resting on the soft, white cotton of his shirt covering his broad back felt the hard, smooth muscles underneath and between her legs she felt a warm sweet tickle of desire.

At the end of the record, she glanced up at him briefly and returned to the table. Not a word had been spoken but they both knew something had changed. So did a number of other people. The moment she sat down, Richard asked her for a dance and she accepted. He held her close and his hand slid down her back. Laughing she pushed him away from her and forced him to dance a mock waltz in order to keep him under control. Around the room tongues were clicking, whispers were spreading. Speculations were made about the change in Rachel Drummond. Nothing definite, she had danced with so many different men. And she used to be so quiet. She was always attractive. Yes, but she never used to dress like that. She does look good. But doesn't she know it. Something is going to happen there. And her husband is such a nice man. Works away from home a lot. Oh.

Then suddenly they were all distracted. Dave Stevens had been dancing with a young, attractive nurse and was standing at the edge of the room talking to her. The cool immaculate Eleanor had had enough and striding over, she slapped Dave around the face and told the other woman to 'Fuck off and leave my husband alone.' The young woman burst into tears, Dave grabbed Eleanor by the wrist and yanked her across the room and outside. Rachel Drummond was forgotten;

this was much more scandalous. 'My god! Did you see that?' 'Did you hear the language?'

Richard and Rachel returned to the table to find out what had happened. Kathy filled them in dismissing the incident with, 'Some people can't take their drink.' As Richard sat down, Gillian put a possessive hand on his arm and Rachel realised that she was jealous. Gillian laughed slightly falsely and said she was going to ask Martin for a dance but she didn't think she was strong enough to carry him. Hearing his name being mentioned Martin raised his chin off his chest and said,

'Dance, do you want to dance, Gillian?'

'No, it's okay, thanks Martin.'

'Ah good,' and his chin slumped forward again. They all laughed and Kathy said 'I think maybe it's time to go home.'

As they waited for taxis, Dave and Eleanor came past. Her hair was dishevelled, make-up smeared and a lot of hissed, venomous language was being exchanged.

'Not such a perfect couple after all,' remarked Kathy cynically.

Kathy and George shared with Rachel and Martin going via their house first so that George could help get Martin safely inside. Martin decided he wanted to lie down on the sofa and no amount of persuasion would change his mind so they took off his shoes, put a pillow under his head, a blanket over him, and left him cuddling the plaque that he had won. Rachel went to bed thinking about Gary. She felt warm and sensuous as she remembered the dance. A little voice told her it was wrong but she was intoxicated with alcohol and a lovely feeling, so fell asleep enjoying her desire in the knowledge that it was reciprocated.

Chapter 21

Four hours later, she was up getting the children their breakfast and the post-drinking depression and guilt began to take away those good feelings. She thought about the incident with Gordon Jones and groaned with regret. Suddenly, she felt as if she had danced too much, made a fool of herself. She thought of Gary and the emotions of warmth and tingling desire were replaced by feeling ridiculous and certain that everyone had noticed.

She put a video on for Max and Lauren and told them she was going back to bed for a while. Thank God, they were at an age where they could entertain themselves for an hour or so. Martin had made his way up to bed at some point in the early hours so Rachel climbed back in next to him. She curled up on her side facing away from him hoping the remorse for the night before would melt away. It felt as though she'd barely closed her eyes before someone was shaking her awake again. It was Max and it was ten o'clock. Martin was already up. 'Come on, Mum, we're going in the desert.' She reached out and drew him towards her for a cuddle which he allowed her to do for a couple of seconds and then he started pulling off the duvet saying 'Come on, get up Mummy, get up.'

'All right, all right,' she laughed. 'Give me another cuddle first,' and she sat on the edge of the bed and pulled him to her. He tried to pull away protesting, so she started to tickle him until he was giggling uncontrollably and calling out for her to stop. She ruffled his hair and gave him a kiss. 'Right, Mummy's up. I'll be downstairs in a tick. Where's Daddy?'

'He's packing the cool box,' Max said running out of the room.

Rachel had bought all the food the day before and made up a container of Pimms so it didn't take long to get ready to leave. She took a paracetamol to calm her throbbing head and had three cups of tea before starting to feel relatively normal. The weather report had said there would be high winds off shore so they'd arranged to go out Wadi bashing with friends rather than on the boats. When it was too rough to go boating, it was perfect weather for going inland with a cool breeze blowing.

They met up with Althea and Joe Richter, Gillian and Richard and waited for Peter and Jane to arrive with their friend, Andrew, who knew the wadis like the back of his hand. Peter and Andrew eventually arrived but Jane had not been feeling well enough to go bouncing across dry river beds so had decided to stay home. Everyone was subdued, jaded from the night before apart from the four children who were excited and impatient. They set off and, as the scenery changed from the drab, flat stretches of dull beige dotted with struggling vegetation to rising dunes of orange and golden sand, their spirits rose.

Each dune reached to a peak like the crest of a wave; a sharp line between where wind had driven the grains upward on a smooth curve on one side and a flatter, steeper face on the other. Dune upon dune of soft, pure sand undulated into the distance. The children screeched in delight every time they spotted a group of camels near the roadside. These creatures stood indolently in the landscape as if placed there in the middle of nowhere without purpose. They held up haughty heads with a look of total indifference at passers-by and an expression around their mouths of sneering disdain. The dunes began to make way for mountains, small eruptions of grey, slanting rock, that looked as if they had been laid sideways, stood relentless on their left hand side. In the distance, rows of peaks stood out of the haze like cardboard cut outs placed one behind the other ranging from dark grey at the front to mauve and pink in the background. It was like an illustration from a book of fairy tales. Every so often, they would pass an oasis of rich, verdant vegetation, lush and bright in the midst of the greys, blacks and browns of the rocky ground.

They turned off the main highway and onto a single track that swept down a steep valley and then up and around. Twisting and turning with dips and rises, each car threw up a trail of dust so they had to spread out in order to see where they were going. Coming to the top of a rise, you could not see what the road was like on the other side. More often than not, it was an even steeper drop. Each time they drove up, there was a rush of anxiety and exhilaration followed by shouts and whoops as they sped down the other side. Rachel joined in with the children's enthusiasm and delight.

A sharp turn to the right took them into the riverbed. The cars lumbered over small rocks and stones trying to avoid the larger boulders that had been swept down during the wet season and deposited on the now dry riverbed. The banks grew higher and the bed narrower as they passed into a gorge with high grey walls of rock towering up on either side of their four wheel drives. The engines revved and roared, suspensions bounced, pushed to their limits as the boulders became more pronounced. Then the gorge widened out again, giving way to a wide shingle base with rocks and boulders piled up on either side.

They came to a stop at the edge of a small pool. A stream of clear, shallow water led from that pool to another, larger and deeper, surrounded by a semi-circle of rock. From a gap in the far wall came a cascade of water, falling from pools higher up. During the rainy season, these innocent looking pools of water could become part of a raging torrent of water. Gushing down from the mountains and filling the gorge at tremendous speed, they could be lethal. These 'flash' floods swept everything in their path downwards and people had been caught out, sometimes losing their lives.

Today there was no risk of that and they all

unloaded cool boxes and changed into swimming gear. Pinter charged around wagging his tail and picking up new and interesting scents. The children ran splashing along the stream into the bigger pool; shallow at the edge it dropped into a seemingly bottomless hole. The water was bitingly cold at first and then gloriously comfortable as the body accustomed itself to the temperature around it. Joe prepared the barbecue and cans of beer and glasses of wine were offered around and accepted – hangovers forgotten or the need for a hair of the dog.

They all swapped stories about the night before; outfits and hairstyles were ripped apart, and various personalities pulled to pieces. They laughed at Martin falling asleep and at Rachel knocking beer over Gordon Jones. She said that she wished she had poured it over Martin for joining in with Gordon and immediately regretted it. Everyone laughed but she knew she meant it and Martin knew she meant it and would pick a fight later. Everything he said or did that day irritated her. At one point, he came over to her, put his arm around her shoulder and pecked her on the cheek and she almost winced but managed to cover it by calling to Lauren to come and have something to eat.

Max and Lauren fell asleep in the car on the way back and Rachel and Martin lifted them out and put them to bed. A long time ago, she and Martin would have snuggled up on the sofa to spend a quiet hour together discussing the week but Rachel busied herself with emptying the cool box and to her relief he announced that he was going straight to bed.

Chapter 22

Saturday evening Rachel played squash with Gillian. Afterwards, as they sat on the veranda overlooking the brightly lit tennis courts, Gillian brought up Thursday night and asked her if she had enjoyed herself. Rachel said she had thoroughly enjoyed it.

'Martin was in a bit of a state. I don't think I've seen him that drunk before. Was he all right?' she continued.

'He'd had a few at the sailing club before we went out so he was already on the way. I left him sleeping on the couch with his award when we got back.'

'Is everything all right between you?'

'Yes its fine,' Rachel replied a little over emphatically.

'You seem to get on very well with Gary.'

'Oh Gary. We've become quite good friends through the show. He's really kind,' she said trying to sound casual.

'Sometimes friendships can lead to more,' said Gillian, 'I should know.' She looked hard at Rachel.

Rachel laughed and said, 'Don't worry. Martin and I are fine, and Gary and I are just friends. I'm pretty sure he's still in love with his ex-wife actually. Listen it's my birthday this Thursday – the big three-o will you and Richard come out to celebrate?'

'Oh is it? Yes, of course we will. Are you worried about reaching thirty?'

Rachel said she hadn't really thought about it, 'It's strange really. I don't feel any different to when I was twenty inside, apart from being a mother, and then I get a vision of my view of thirty when I was a teenager. I remember one of my teachers saying that they were thirty and thinking 'God, how old', and I thought they looked old.' They both laughed.

'I got into a real state about reaching thirty and now I'm on the way to forty it doesn't seem to matter anymore,' said Gillian.

'Thirty or forty?' laughed Rachel.

'Either. I suppose it depends how satisfied you feel with your life at the time.'

Driving home with a take-away pizza for her and Martin she went over the conversation in her head. She meant what she said, or at least wanted to convince herself she meant it.

At home, she served up the pizza and salad and tried to chat to Martin about the week ahead. She had rehearsals a couple of evenings and Friday afternoon in the run up to the show's first night. He was not pleased.

'And then you'll be doing the show for four nights, I suppose.'

'Yes. Look, it's one week in the year and all I'm asking of you is that you look after Max and Lauren on Friday. You're away all the time and I have to get on with it.'

'That's work to pay for all the things we have and the lifestyle we lead.'

'I work as well and this is the first time I've asked you to put yourself out for me.' She could feel tears welling up and brimming over.

'Oh look don't cry,' he said coming over and putting his arm around her, 'I'm sorry. I'm just not used to you going out all the time. What shall we do on your birthday?'

Rachel smiled through her tears, 'I've invited Gillian and Richard to go out and I thought Kathy, George, Jane and Peter might come too.'

'Okay. Nobody from the choral group you want to invite as well?'

'No, not really.'

'Right, where do you want to go?'

'Let's have Japanese.'

'Whatever you want. Come on let's go to bed.'

He led her upstairs and they cleaned their teeth, got undressed, and climbed under the covers. Martin pulled her to him and whispered that he loved her. 'Love you too,' she replied realising that he hadn't said that to her in along time. They moved together in a natural rhythm, the familiarity with each other's bodies allowing them to flow in a comfortable pattern to arouse and satisfy. She found her thoughts turning to Gary and was shocked by how they excited her. Feeling guilty, she opened her eyes and looked up at Martin with his eyes shut, concentrating on reaching his climax and she felt a sudden disconnect as they went through the motions of lovemaking with something not quite right.

Chapter 23

Rachel went to rehearsal feeling very nervous. They were on stage with lighting, costumes, near enough the full works. There was a buzz of excitement and trepidation. Rachel saw Gary and her stomach flipped over involuntarily. She chatted gaily to other people in the cast and went over to her opposite part, John Govner who was playing Emile de Beque. He was a very serious man, arrogant in the extreme and a perfectionist. Rachel had found him quite difficult, particularly in the love scenes but because he was so particular, he had made her determined to prove that she could do it. She had managed to stop giggling at his rather forced French accent early on, mainly because he couldn't work out what was so funny. They ran through a couple of scenes together before Nick called for a start.

The rehearsal was disastrous and Nick was raging at everyone. In the end, he called it an early night and stormed out saying he hoped people would get their 'act' together for next time. Some people were annoyed at the way he'd spoken to them. Others shrugged and said he was right, they weren't putting everything into it. A few people suggested going to a bar in town and Rachel decided to join them. So did Gary.

It was ladies' night in one of the bars at Le Meridien hotel and so it was packed and lively. As usual, there were at least three men to every woman and the single girls and some married were enjoying plenty of attention. Clusters of men stood drinking and talking, their eyes roving, checking out the female company. Groups of women stood talking, holding onto their complimentary drinks their eyes roving, checking out a likely buyer for the next drink and a possible partner.

Conversation was difficult over loud music unless you bent close to someone and talked into their ear. The crowd from the choral group dissipated into the midst and Rachel found herself alone with Gary. Suddenly, she felt like a teenager as a frisson of desire took her by surprise. As she finished her drink he said, 'Do you want another one or shall we go somewhere else.'

'Go somewhere else,' she replied.

They stepped out of the noise into the cool night.

'Where shall we go?' she asked.

'Well, we could go to another noisy pub or you could come to my flat for a quiet drink.'

'Okay, I'll follow you.'

She watched him walk to his Jaguar XJS admiring his long, strong legs. She got into her car, switched the engine on and her brain off. As she drove along behind him, she could feel her heart against her chest, the muscles in her neck went taut and pulsed. Her hands shook. She should turn off at the next lights. Go home, forget it. But she couldn't. They pulled up outside a large new block of flats on the other side of town. She hadn't been there before. She got out of the car and followed him into the building. They went up in the lift in silence. He opened the door of the flat and she followed him inside. Closing the door and putting down his keys, he checked his answer machine. She felt her heart was going to burst out of her chest.

'What would you like to drink? Gin and Tonic?'

'Yes, thanks,' she said lightly.

He turned to her, took her hand and said 'You're shaking.'

'Yes.'

She looked up into his face; his eyes were soft and full of longing. He took her head in both hands and bent down to kiss her softly on the lips. She responded, hesitatingly at first and then harder. Their lips united, their tongues touched and they melted into one another. He kissed her neck, her shoulders and slowly undid the buttons on her blouse. Moving his mouth down her throat onto her breasts, he removed her shirt and deftly opened her bra pulling the flimsy lace forward over her arms and off. She ran her fingers through his hair and down his back, pulling up his shirt to snake her nails across his shoulders. He paused to pull the shirt over his head and fling it to the floor before running his hands over her breasts, holding them briefly and then moving down to her jeans as his tongue found her nipples and gently sucked them and licked them. He pulled the jeans down over her hips and she kicked off her shoes and finished the removal of all her clothes apart from one item, a black G-string. Her lower body surged with heat, and a warm, sweet wetness between her legs removed any remaining sensible thought in her head. She gave in to her emotions, her physical yearning as his tongue probed behind the cotton into that hidden part of sensuality and her juices flowed. He moved her backwards into the centre of the room and brought her down onto the Persian rug next to the coffee table. Urgently, he pulled off her pants and stood up quickly to remove his jeans and boxer shorts. She closed her eyes not wanting to see all of him and then he was down on top of her. His fingers probed and massaged expertly inside her, hitting the spot and hitting the spot and hitting the spot until her whole body climaxed in a rush of released tension, joy and pleasure. His hard erection pressed against her and she opened up to him. The tip pressed gently against her soft lips, ready for that sweet moment of entrance.

'No.' She pulled backwards, up the rug saying, 'I'm sorry. I'm sorry. I'm so sorry.'

'Hey, hey. It's all right.'

They sat in the middle of the room, her head buried into his chest, his arms around her holding her.

A muted light from outside sent shades of blue, across the darkened room. There was silence apart from the almost unconscious drone of the air conditioner.

'All right?' he asked huskily, quietly.

'Yes,' she looked at him and smiled. 'That was so, so lovely. I'm so sorry.' She sighed from deep within her soul.

'There's no rush. I'm sorry, I thought it was what you wanted.'

She didn't speak. She couldn't explain how right it felt and how wrong. Then she looked at the time on the huge Swatch watch hung on one column of the room. Reality crept back. It was midnight.

'I'd better go. Where's the loo?'

She tried to laugh as she pulled on her clothes but it sounded unnatural. In the bathroom, she looked at her flushed face and tousled hair in the mirror. Going back through, she found him sitting on the chair near to the window in his boxer shorts and T-shirt staring out at the sky. She went over to him nervously, knelt at his feet and laid her head on his knee. His hand went out to stroke her hair.

'Looking for the moon?' she asked, looking out at the clear black sky filled with dots of trembling silver.

'Can't see it from here.'

He pulled her up to sit across him and kissed her slowly, sensitively and for a long time, and then held her. It seemed forever but Rachel glancing at the clock was surprised to find that only a few minutes had gone by. She wanted to stay there forever, to forget what had just happened, to just be there with him holding her, to hold onto this precious moment before stepping back into real life where she knew they would never be able to hold each other again. But the clock had already taken it.

'I must go.'

'I'll ring you at work tomorrow.'

'Yes.'

'You're very special.'

'Thank you.'

She kissed him and left as if in a dream. She walked coolly out of the building and to her car. Driving home, she felt a rush of pleasure low in her abdomen each time she thought of Gary combined with the growing tension of deceit. She hadn't gone all the way but she had wanted to. She was numb with confusion. She couldn't allow herself to think about what would happen next.

She arrived home and Martin was watching TV. She had hoped he would be in bed.

'Hi!' she said as nonchalantly as possible but felt it ring falsely high pitched.

'That was a long rehearsal. How'd it go?'

'Awful. Nick threw a wobbly. Everybody was rubbish. Do you want a coffee?' she asked, unable to look at him.

'No, I'm just going up.'

Rachel went into the kitchen without saying anything and put on the kettle. Martin came through and asked, 'Are you okay?'

'Oh I think I'm just getting really nervous about the show. I kept forgetting my lines and I sang awfully tonight.'

It was too much. She started to cry. He gave her a hug and said, 'Is it worth doing this, if it makes you so uptight?' Then he kissed her forehead and said, 'I'm going up, I've got a really busy day tomorrow.'

He left the kitchen and went up the stairs. Rachel suddenly felt so alone. She put coffee in the cup. Got milk out of the fridge. Poured in the water. Poured in a drop of milk. Stirred. Stared ahead at the blind pulled down over the window and let the tears fall. What had happened to them?

Martin brushed his teeth. He felt disconcerted. This bloody show had changed her. She was separate from him, removed somehow. What the hell was the matter with her? He too surged with guilt, which he refused to acknowledge. He'd think about it tomorrow. Right now, he needed to get some sleep.

Chapter 24

Rachel woke up with a start, her stomach lunged and a turbulent, spinning sense of guilt washed up over her, followed by the stabbing joy in her groin. Totally in conflict with one another and yet part of one another she swung between these sensations all morning. There was work to do, but now it seemed more pointless and uninteresting than ever before. All morning she willed Gary to ring. At first, it was with eager anticipation of hearing his voice. By eleven she had a tight knot in her stomach and a feeling of nausea in her throat as she convinced herself that she had been used, a one-night stand was all he'd wanted, a challenge to which she had so nearly succumbed.

The phone rang, she answered automatically in her office voice. His voice came down the line. Her fears melted. They spoke easily, comfortably, their yearning for each other conveyed through tone of voice rather than topic of conversation.

'See you tonight.'

'Yes, bye ... bye'

Rachel picked up the children as usual and took them home. She watched them as they ate their lunch oblivious to the way their mother was feeling, to what she was doing. She was overwhelmed with love for them and asked herself what she was doing but had no power to stop. She got through the day and the night and the next day on another planet, held together by three calls from Gary at work.

She left for rehearsal on Tuesday before Martin got home. This was the first full run through on the stage. Everyone was excitable; the nerves were really beginning to show through now.

She and Gary behaved as normal towards each other but as she waited alone in the wings for her entrance he brushed his lips across the back of her neck as he passed by. The quivering sensation that sped through her nearly made her miss her entrance but on she went. She was so well rehearsed that everything fell into place once she was out in front with the rest of the cast. When she came off, he grinned at her and she punched him on the arm trying to be annoyed.

At the end of the evening, he walked out to the car park with her. They had done this before but now suddenly there was the feeling of eyes everywhere. People could see that things had changed between them; they had huge great signs on their backs declaring to the world. Suddenly he grabbed her hand and led her quickly, silently to the beach beyond the car park. Rachel glanced around in panic but saw no one. Once on the soft sand, he pulled her to him and kissed her full and hard on the mouth. Oh that kiss, so sweet, so long, as if their lips were made for one another. He laid her gently down on his jacket and as the sea whispered he removed her clothes, caressed her body and made love to her slowly, sensitively surely, and more surely, watching her, waiting for her and then together, together, together.

They lay briefly holding each other but the cool breeze caused them to shiver and it was getting late. They dressed subduing their laughter as they tried to get rid of the pervasive sand and he held her to kiss her once more before returning to the car park. At her car, they kissed politely on both cheeks and she got in. She wound down the window and he said, 'I'm in love with you and I want you. I don't know how we'll work it out but I have to be honest because when you find something like this, you don't let it go. I'm free. You're married with children. If you don't feel the same, stop it now. Come up to my office tomorrow when you've finished. 1603. Bye.'

He walked quickly away. She felt like a medicine ball had smashed into her guts. Every inch of her strained to go after him to be with him but she couldn't move. She sat in the car, staring ahead, unable to think clearly. She drove home. Martin was asleep. She showered quickly in the children's bathroom, brushed the sand out of hair and put her clothes in the laundry basket. Her heart thumped, she prayed Martin wouldn't wake. She went into the children and stood standing at the edge of their beds watching their smooth, carefree faces in innocent sleep. Quietly, she changed for bed and lay awake. She looked at Martin, his normally neat hair ruffled, his face too, like a child's, peaceful in sleep. She wanted to reach out and cuddle him, comfort him for the pain she would cause him. She lay for hours unable to switch off but not thinking logically, her brain running off at tangents. What was she doing? The call to prayer came and went before she finally slept.

Chapter 25

In the morning, she got up and went through the motions of organising the children, making their breakfast and hurrying them out to the car. She dropped them off at school and set off in the direction of the office. Suddenly, she decided that she couldn't face work. She went back to the house and phoned in sick. It was the first day off she had ever taken. Junata looked puzzled, 'You okay Madam?'

'Not really, Junata. I'm going to take Pinter out for a walk.'

'Okay, madam.' The smiling Sri Lankan wobbled her head in a slight gesture of 'Whatever you say,' and moved in her calm, unhurried fashion towards the kitchen.

Rachel took Pinter to the beach. She drove onto the soft white sand and stopped about twenty yards from the water's edge. The long curving beach with the Hilton in the distance was deserted. Huge white and grey clouds swam across the sky, a cool wind whipped

QUICKSAND

across the top of the sea setting it in motion in its irreversible movement towards the beach, ending in the crash and slap against the shore and then followed by the mournful sigh as it drew breath and crashed and splashed again. Rachel let the breeze caress her face and hair as she sat down on the pale gold sand and gazed at the sea and sky conscious of the colours, the blends of varying blues and white and grey and its total beauty. The never-ending changing movement of clouds and water and yet they always remained. The inconstant constancy struck her heart as she struggled with herself.

Her stomach ached, not with pain, but with grappling, swirling emotions. Her chest felt stretched and tight and there was a recurring spring of yearning that seemed to recoil for short periods and then shoot out from the very pit of her, up through her gullet, to the back of her throat. She stood up and began to walk along the water's edge.

She took deep breaths, she'd been here before, felt this way before but that had been because somebody had left her, not because they wanted her. She felt nothing but confusion. How had she got to this point? Why had she got there? Where had the comfortable complacency and general satisfaction gone? Could she step back? Should she go forwards? She thought about Gary and had to shut her eyes as the strength of feeling caught her breath.

She thought about Martin and the children and felt so sad. She thought of other people and how they would view it. Another scandal to rock their fragile foundations. Another juicy piece of gossip to frown over, gasp over, dine on for a few weeks. If only you could rip open your skin and reveal the gremlins eating away at your sense and sensibility. What guarantee did you have that if you moved on, that it would be better? Weren't all relationships the same? The fireworks, the extremes of emotion and then the compromise of everyday living and the levelling off into vague companionship and comfortability. Surely, it was better to work at what you'd got than to be disillusioned by romance.

Yes, it was a madness.

Rachel stood still and turned with determination, she took a deep breath and, calling Pinter, made her way back along the empty beach to the car. She had been nearly two hours. Now she had to get past midday without giving in to the urge to go to Gary. She put Pinter in the back and stepped round to get in noticing that the sand was softer than she had realised. She got in, started the engine and pressed the accelerator. The car moved forward and then stopped. She pressed the accelerator again and heard the engine straining. Her heart went into her mouth. She put it into four-wheel drive and tried reversing, but the wheels were just spinning in the sand and the engine was screaming. 'Damn, damn!" she said, banging the steering wheel with the palm of her hands.

She got out to take a look and saw the back wheels almost half covered in soft sand. Looking desperately around, there was nobody in sight, so she began digging, trying to move some of the sand away from the wheels in a futile attempt to free them. The sweat was pouring down her face, mixed with tears of frustration. The sound of a car made her step back and she looked up to see an Arab in a Toyota Land Cruiser tearing along the beach at speed towards her. He parked next to her and got out. He was a handsome young man in a sparkling white kandura; on his head he wore an equally clean and white gutra held in place by the usual black agal. His eyes were hidden by designer sunglasses. He flicked the white headscarf over his shoulders and came over to her with a smile. Taking off his sunglasses, he asked, 'Do you need some help?' in a clear English accent.

Rachel looked at his smooth brown skin and deep dark eyes and nodded, 'Ugh, yes, please. So silly of me! I could do with a tow.'

He replaced his sunglasses, grinned at her and, ignoring the barking Pinter, he jumped into the driving seat and turned on the engine. He put the car in drive, then reverse, drive and reverse a few times, and the car seemed to rock forward and backwards in the heavy sand. Then, with a sharp press on the accelerator, the car rolled smoothly forward and out of the rut. He drove it round in a loop, came to a stop on the hard, flat sand at the top of the beach, and got out. She walked over to him with an embarrassed smile on her face and said, 'Thank you! That was incredible.'

He replied with, 'Al hamd'Allah,' and went casually back to his own car. He drove slowly past her and she waved and mouthed 'shukran'. He raised his hand, grinned again and accelerated forward to continue his fun racing along the thick sandy part of the beach.

She took a deep breath and set off for home. In her panic, she had stopped thinking about everything else. Back at home, she made a cup of tea and thoughts of Gary began creeping in again. She would go just to talk to him, to explain. No. They could still be friends, what a shame if that good friendship was to be ruined. Her mind twisted and turned. She could not think straight. She phoned Jane. No answer. She phoned Kathy at work. They talked briefly, arranged where to meet on Thursday. Rachel spoke normally, cheerfully. Kathy was busy, they said goodbye.

Eleven. She tried Jane again. She answered.

'Hi, Jane. It's Rachel. How are you?'

'Not so good actually. I've had some strange pains across my tummy. I've got a check-up this afternoon.'

'Shall I come over?' asked Rachel.

'Would you? I'm getting into a bit of a silly panic. I know I'm worrying about nothing but come over. It will take my mind off it. Hang on. Why aren't you at work?'

'Oh I woke up feeling terrible but I'm okay now and bored.'

'See you in a while then. Bye.'

Rachel's stomach seemed to roll over and over. She grabbed her handbag and sunglasses and left the house. Damn! She'd left the car keys inside. She rang the bell and waited for Junata.

'Forgot my keys,' she laughed.

Junata shrugged and went back to the housework. Rachel arrived at Jane's in a daze. It was quarter past eleven. Gritting her teeth, she went up to Jane and Peter's apartment and rang the bell. Jane came to the door. She looked terrible, her face was pallid and frightened.

'Jane! Are you all right?' Stupid question.

'It comes and goes Rachel. Aah!' she bent double clutching her stomach 'Oh God! Help me!' Tears of pain and fear streamed down her face.

'Come on. We've got to get you to the hospital,' said Rachel forgetting everything else.

The wave of pain relented and Jane allowed Rachel to guide her downstairs and into the car. They went straight to emergency and three nurses took control of the situation. Calm, straightforward, efficient they took Jane away. It was twenty to twelve. Rachel rang Peter and without alarming him, told him Jane was in the hospital and asked if he could come to fetch her. The lack of urgency in her voice unfortunately made him question if it was necessary to come straight away.

'Listen Peter, I don't want to worry you, but I suggest you get down here as fast as possible.'

'Oh God! Right, I'm on my way.'

Rachel went back to the emergency reception to see if they could tell her anything.

'No just wait here. Is the father coming?'

'Yes, he's on his way.'

She sat down, stood up, walked around. Sat down, stood up, walked around. Noted the time, ten to twelve. All she wanted to do was call Gary, have Gary there to put his arms around her, 'Please don't let her lose the baby,' she prayed silently.

Peter arrived anxious, confused, 'What's happening? Where is she?'

Rachel explained what had happened and led him through to one of the nurses who took him to see Jane. Rachel said she would wait. She went to the phone. Every sense in her pulled her towards ringing Gary. She started to dial. No. She put the phone down and rang Martin. He was in a meeting. She rang Althea Richter to ask if she could pick up the children, briefly explaining what was happening, then the school to let them know Althea was to take Max and Lauren. She hovered by the phone, a lump in her throat, her heart heaving, her hand shaking. Then she thought about Jane and concentrated on her friend's agony. In her mind, she imagined Gary somehow knowing where she was and rushing in. She went to the desk again. It was twenty past twelve. He would know she wasn't coming. Maybe he'd rung before and knew she hadn't been at work.

While she waited, a continual stream of people passed through the reception area. Excited fathers arrived on their way to visit a new baby with the extended family of grandma, grandpa, uncles, aunts, sisters, brothers, chattering animatedly; little girls proudly dressed in elaborate party dresses with ruffles, frills, bows and sashes. Others left pushing trolleys laden with huge bouquets of plastic flowers and bowls of sweets.

A group of Muslim women covered from head to toe in flowing black robes arrived all talking at once, wailing as they rushed one of them into emergency; which of them was pregnant was impossible to tell.

Rachel started reading the various posters on the wall giving advice on pregnancy and childbirth and was amused by a large one saying:

Backache, nausea, tiredness, headaches, heartburn and constipation are all NORMAL during pregnancy.

'So don't complain' thought Rachel cynically shaking her head. She rose and went up to the desk again.

'Any news of Jane Matthews?'

The nurse made a call and Rachel heard her say, 'Ah that's good news.'

A wave of relief washed over Rachel. The nurse put the phone down and smiled. 'She's fine, the baby's fine. They're keeping her in for observation. Probably indigestion.'

'Indigestion!' Rachel laughed but knew she was on the brink of tears. She went up to the ward and met Peter coming out of Jane's room. She went up to him and put her arms around his chest. He hugged into her and she started to cry.

'Jesus,' he said, 'it's strange but I don't think I realised how much I want this baby until now, or how much I love Jane.'

They looked at each other, 'I know,' said Rachel then they burst out laughing.

'Fucking indigestion! She's sleeping now. Come on, I'll buy you a drink,' said Peter.

Rachel phoned Junata to tell her she'd be back about two and went to the bar in the Club to meet Peter. The amazing jungle drums had been beating and people immediately came up to ask how Jane was. You couldn't keep bad news down. They all expressed relief but with a few people, Rachel couldn't help noting a tinge of disappointment at it being a false alarm.

The bar was not busy. An English man in his forties sat with his young Filippino wife at one table eating snacks and not talking to one another. A group of English guys stood joking, drinking at one end of the bar. A regular sat alone on his usual stool at the other end drinking pints and exchanging a few words with anyone who stood near enough, long enough. At one table, six or seven Arabs sat in their white dish-dash. Two English women, heavily made-up and laden with jewellery sat with them laughing and flirting. They were well known for mixing with the Arabs on a more than friendly basis – often exchanging favours in the back of their Mercedes in the car park for gifts of gold. Sri Lankan and Indian waiters moved between the tables changing ashtrays, clearing glasses and taking orders. Rachel and Peter ordered drinks and Peter lit a cigarette, inhaled deeply and sat back blowing the smoke up into the air in a long exhalation of breath.

Gary had phoned Rachel's office and knew she wasn't there. His heart had dropped but he'd waited in hope that she may arrive anyway. It had been a long time since he'd felt this way. He thought about her body, the touch of her skin and the way she had responded to him. Her thick, short cropped hair and wide eyes. He knew deep down she felt the same but also knew about the bonds of marriage. He'd sensed her discontentment and vulnerability but hadn't meant to take advantage. He enjoyed her company and her friendship. Maybe he'd rushed it. Maybe he should have given it more time. As the clock ticked by, he began to close down his heart. He hadn't slept the night before for thinking about Rachel and how much he wanted her and how it might work out. At one, he left and drove to the Club to check on scenery. He saw her car in the car park and his stomach turned over. As he walked past the bar, he caught sight of her and kept on going. He didn't think she'd seen him. He carried on to the backstage entrance; all his old training came to the fore. Cover emotions; control over fear and sorrow, and nervousness. A couple of the crew were there. He spoke normally, made a few jokes, and threw himself into the job at hand.

Rachel had seen him. What should she do? Should she go and talk to him now or wait until tonight? If she didn't speak to him soon they might never be friends again. Could they still be friends? She didn't think he'd seen her as he walked past the bar. Better to leave it until the rehearsal when everyone was around. Or should she go now and try to explain?

'Are you okay, Rachel?' asked Peter.

'Oh yes sorry, I was just thinking about Jane, and about myself when I was pregnant.'

'It's a funny time isn't it? But so good the way it makes your relationship stronger because of the difficulty.'

'Well I never thought I'd hear you say something like that,' Rachel laughed.

They got their drinks and a sandwich and chatted about what changes Peter could expect in his life. He seemed genuinely interested in all the different aspects of childbirth and having a young child. They laughed about Jane's indigestion and joked about her being a midwife and not knowing what was wrong.

'I'm going back to the hospital now, see if Jane's woken up so I can tease her,' laughed Peter.

'Don't you dare! And remember she'll have to take it easy. I'd better go home and see Max and Lauren. I've got to leave early for rehearsal tonight.'

'How's the show going? Can't wait to see you doing your Mitzi Gaynor impression.'

'I am impressed that you know the name of the actress who played my part.'

'My Mum's favourite film,' Peter shrugged, 'but

didn't she have blonde hair?'

'Yes, I'm dying it tomorrow.'

'Never!'

'No, only joking. There's only so far I'll go for a part.

'Didn't have to sleep with the director, did you?'

Rachel lurched inwardly, 'No, just smiled sweetly and fluttered my eyelashes.'

'Well, have a good rehearsal and thank you. You've been a great friend today.'

'I'm just glad everything's okay. I was worried sick.'

They left the bar together and went out to the car park. Rachel drove home. She thought about Martin and how good he'd been during both her pregnancies, loving, interested, and so supportive. She pictured his proud face as he'd held up each child after the birth and squeezed her hand. She thought of Gary and felt the pulling need for him but willed it to go away. Her throat tightened and the tears came. Pulling into a side street, she stopped the car and sobbed. A couple of Indian workmen in drab baggy clothes stopped and stared but she could not have cared. Her shoulders shook and her chest heaved as she cried for Sylvia and for Gary and for herself.

When Martin came home, she told him about Jane. He found it hilarious and she felt that somehow he'd missed all the worry and fear they had gone through.

Chapter 26

At the next rehearsal she was overly friendly and bouncy with everyone. She took a deep breath, went over to Gary, and said 'Hello'. He said hello back with an edge of coolness. Rachel started talking, too quickly, too brightly about nothing in particular. He listened, responded, and then said he had to get backstage and walked away. Rachel felt sick, embarrassed, and lost. She pulled herself together; she had a role to play. It was semi-dress so she changed and allowed someone to try out the stage make-up on her. She laughed at any jokes made, responded to questions and comments, but was not really there. She felt removed, not quite a part of all the hustle and bustle around. Every so often, she caught sight of Gary directing scenery changes and in control of backstage procedure and the ache in her stomach grew.

Nick gave them all a talk. This was his last rehearsal. After tonight, they had the dress rehearsals when the Stage Manager would take charge and then there would be a paying audience who deserved to get their money's worth. Rachel started to feel anxious. She realised that she had been so distracted that she had forgotten about doing the show for real in front of a live audience.

The rehearsal started and she concentrated on getting everything right. Each time she came into the wings she looked for Gary but he was never on her side. She missed his smile, his encouragement. Oh, how she wanted him to kiss the back of her neck again. When it came to 'I'm Gonna Wash that Man Right out of my Hair' she sang with such feeling that everyone commented and congratulated her. At the end, Nick was pleased, for the first time in weeks he sounded enthusiastic, excited.

'We have a great show, thank you everybody – a few technical hitches to sort out but now I know it'll be fantastic on the night.'

Everyone hummed with pleasure. Mary Watson went over each of her scenes in a loud, proud voice – how she'd nearly done this but had managed to cover it and how she'd covered for lines missed by other characters. The chorus, relaxed and bubbling, were still singing their songs. Rachel changed and joined everyone in the bar. She couldn't see Gary. Someone suggested going to one of the nightclubs and Rachel still on a high from the adrenalin of performing decided to join them. She offered a lift to Maggie and Ron Timmings. Ron was playing Luther Billis and he was a natural comedian. He kept them laughing all the way across town. As they got out of the car, Rachel said,

'Hey its nearly my birthday what's the time?'

'Your birthday? Why didn't you tell anyone? Come on let's go and celebrate!' cried Ron. They entered the dark club. The loud, throbbing music seemed to take them over, flashing lights across the disco floor and gyrating bodies filled them with a living rhythm. They joined the rest of the crowd and Ron shouted to everybody that it was Rachel's birthday. Champagne was ordered and they stopped the disco to get everyone to sing 'Happy Birthday'. Everyone gave her a kiss and then they all threw themselves into dancing as the music resumed. Rachel pushed everything out of her mind and danced and laughed and drank. At three in the morning, she left to share a taxi with a couple of the school teachers. They dropped her off at the villa and she waved goodbye before fumbling in her handbag for door keys. She couldn't quite see straight as she tried to get the right key in the hole. She pushed the door open and nearly tripped over the step. She giggled and told herself to concentrate. Closing the door gently, she misjudged the distance and it banged shut. 'Shh' she said to it. Turning around she came face to face with Martin.

'Where the bloody hell have you been!' he snarled.

'Shh, Shh,' Rachel said, 'That is a very naughty door. Did you hear it bang? I told it to be quiet but it just didn't listen.' She giggled again.

'Rachel!'

'It's my birthday. Can I have a birthday kiss?' She put her arms around him. He tried to stay angry but could see it was pointless. She was also very funny.

He helped her upstairs as she missed nearly every step and said 'Ooh it moved. Why do the stairs keep moving? We'd better ring the postman. No, not the postman the land- landlord, that's the one.'

He helped her undress. She fell on the bed saying, 'It's my birthday, I'm really horny,' and fell fast asleep.

Lauren and Max rushed into the bedroom in the morning to wish Mummy 'Happy Birthday' and give her their homemade cards. Mummy was very pleased but did not feel too good. She groaned all the way through showering and getting dressed.

'Serves you right,' said Martin as he did up his tie. 'What the bloody hell were you doing last night?'

'Aren't you going to wish me happy birthday?' she replied.

'Rachel. What are you doing?'

'I'm having a good time. I'm sorry I was late, we were all on a high after rehearsal and then they all insisted on celebrating my birthday.'

'So are you going to be doing the same for the next week?'

'I don't know, probably not – I think I'd die.'

Martin was frustrated, he felt out of control. She seemed so sure of herself and as if she couldn't care less of him. 'Fine if that's the way you want it!' he said brusquely.

Rachel went over to him and cuddled him, 'Don't be angry. I'll see you later and we'll have a good time together tonight.'

'I was worried about you.'

'I know. I am sorry.'

She kissed him. He left for work.

She felt remorseful. She was feeling good and in control because she had made up her mind but of course Martin didn't know what she'd been going through. She'd make it up to him that night.

They went out with Kathy and George, Richard and Gillian and Peter. Jane was still in the hospital for rest and observation but all the scans and tests had showed the baby to be fine. Rachel was exhausted, but knew she couldn't admit to it. Luckily, Kathy and George were on excellent form and kept up lively conversation throughout the meal. Martin was subdued. He had come home with flowers and a gold necklace for her present but was not quite sure of her. Rachel worked hard at showing him affection and attention but it became more difficult as the evening went on and he made odd references to the night before, subtle digs about the choral group and 'Rachel the star'. She laughed them off but was hurt. Everyone made an effort, a cake arrived, they sang 'Happy Birthday' but the evening didn't get off the ground. They finished the meal at midnight and vague suggestions about going on were made but no one's heart was really in it. They all parted company.

Martin announced that he was going to bed and Rachel said she was too. In bed she turned to him and whispered 'Thank you for my present. I love you.' He didn't say anything. 'Can I have my proper present now?' She stretched her hand out across his belly and stroked down to take hold of him. He moved, pecked her on the cheek, said 'Maybe tomorrow if you're good,' and turned his back to her. She felt the knife cut her deep inside and twist.

Chapter 27

The technical dress rehearsal was due to start at three, everyone was to be there for costumes and make up around two. It was a beautiful day, a very slight breeze and cloudless sky. Martin announced in the morning that he would take the children and Pinter out on the boat with people from the sailing club. Rachel made them sandwiches, packed the cool box and the swimming bag and they left at midday.

'Bye Mummy!'

'Bye Mummy. Good luck Mummy!'

Rachel went back into the house, closed the door, and leant back against it. Quiet. A rare occasion when she was alone in the house, without even Pinter to disturb the peace by barking at cats. She drew in a deep breath and closed her eyes. Her stomach flipped and somersaulted. She tried to put it down to nerves for the coming performances but knew that wasn't all. Going to the bar, she made a stiff gin and tonic and went out to sit on the veranda in the comfortable sunshine. Martin hadn't even wished her luck. Why did he resent her being in the show? She thought of Gary and was shocked by the force of the sharp rush from low down up to her throat like a gust from an Egyptian Khamsin, hot and oppressive. She willed herself not to want him, not to think about him as anything but a good friend. She knew things had changed irreversibly for her and that she would not fit back into the neat pigeon hole Martin and others had posted her in but she did not want to destroy the family unit. She could work it out with Martin, he would understand that she needed more, maybe she could find another job which demanded more intellectual stimulus. Thoughts, plans whirled in her head, by the time she had to set off for the Club she felt confident, sure of her future. As she drove along she went over her lines and nervous excitement filled her. She hoped she wouldn't crumble in front of the audience of school parties invited for the matinee dress rehearsal.

She went into the dressing room where people were fiddling with costumes, complaining about this and that, and an harassed looking wardrobe lady was making last minute alterations. Others were putting on make-up or having it applied. Chorus members were organising kitties for a supply of drinks to get them through the performance, laughing and joking under a façade of being relaxed. Main characters went over lines together or paced up and down not talking to anyone. Rachel got ready, her reaction to the nervous tension was to chatter gaily when anyone spoke to her and then relapse into concentrated effort to calm the bats in her stomach.

Everything was ready; everyone was waiting for the

curtain to open. Standing in the wings waiting for her first entrance her whole body shook, her throat felt dry and tight, she didn't know if she wanted to pee, or be sick. God, why was she doing this? What masochistic tendencies made people put themselves in this position? She looked up and caught Gary looking at her from the opposite side of the stage. He smiled at her and mouthed 'smile' at her serious, worried face. She smiled, her cue came, and she was on.

The bright lights glared and she was vaguely aware of a number of people, eyes fixed on the stage, on her, in the darkness behind the flood of brightness. And then she was saying her lines and into the character, in the part. Her body no longer shook, the adrenalin flowed, and she spoke clearly, confidently. She forgot the dryness in her throat, as her songs came across like sweet, flowing honey. When the curtain closed at the end to enthusiastic applause, she knew why people put themselves in this position. Her whole body buzzed. What a high!

The whole cast was caught up in the general feeling of the pleasure of success. Everyone congratulated everyone else. Of course, they'd all known it would be good. Nick beamed as he patted everyone on the back. Drinks flowed and the chorus girls sang and danced as Ron acted the fool and gave impersonations of famous characters including spotty dog from the Wooden Tops.

Gary gave Rachel a hug and congratulated her. She held her glass up to him and said, 'Thank you.' They held each other's eyes briefly in understanding. A pang of desire passed swiftly across her chest mixed with relief. She felt sure she'd made the right decision and filled with warmth knowing that she and Gary would still be friends. It was right. Everything was in its correct place. They had the next day off and then one more dress rehearsal before the actual run began on Monday night.

Martin was watching television when she came in. She was lively, elated and excited. He misinterpreted her, felt hurt and anger knocking his heart as he realised her behaviour was due to something separate from him. She bounced into his lap and asked him how his day had gone. He answered flatly, indifferently. She refused to let him bring her down. He didn't ask about the show so Rachel told him, describing her nervousness, what had happened on and off stage and the audience reaction. Her words bubbled out and she could hardly keep still. She cuddled and cajoled him until he softened and managed to say he was pleased for her.

'I'm sorry Rache. I've had a hard couple of weeks at work. I'm looking forward to seeing the last night performance and I do hope it goes well.' He gave her a hug. He wanted to say more, she wanted to say more but no words seemed to come out.

'I'm going to get an early night,' he finally said and kissed her before going off up the stairs. Rachel was still hyperactive; she went to the bar and poured herself a brandy. Things were not right. A sharp jolt of guilt went through her. May be it was her fault; she couldn't deny her thoughts and her actions where Gary was concerned. Suddenly there seemed to be a huge, gaping chasm between her and Martin. They used to talk over everything, say how they were feeling, get niggles and annoyances cleared away. Now it seemed that they hadn't done that for a long, long time and that what may have started as a tiny fissure had been left to widen and deepen. Could they close the gap? Of course they could, there was too much to lose. Everybody went through bad patches. She was too pleased with herself and the show to feel pessimistic. As soon as the show was over, they could work at it. Christmas was coming, they could sort it out then. The brandy warmed her and dulled her senses, she went to bed happy.

Chapter 28

Saturday she slept in. She was more exhausted than she realised and her sleep had been filled with strange dreams. She hadn't even been aware of Martin getting up and leaving with the children. She lay in bed trying to remember what she had dreamt about and suddenly she caught a snatch, someone had broken into the house dressed in black, she'd been trying to fight them off and had pulled off the black hood to reveal a woman. Again, she had been trying to push her away but had no strength to lift her arms. As she remembered, she felt the same sense of weakness she had experienced in the dream. Shaking off the feeling, she got up, showered and went down to make herself a coffee.

She decided she needed to spend more time with the children and felt guilty for neglecting them the day before. She was cross about the guilt, it wasn't often she left them and they had been with their father for God's sake. 'I want to spend time with them,' she thought.

It was a glorious November day. The Club was packed with people. Children screamed and splashed in the pool, glistening bodies relaxed in the warmth and groups sat around eating and drinking as the waiters rushed around trying to keep up with the orders. Rachel had fun swimming and playing with Max and Lauren and took them home worn out from an active afternoon. As she got them into bed and read to them, she felt calm and peaceful. She dismissed the pang of guilt she felt, and was thankful that she'd put an end to things before they'd gone any further. She put it all down to a moment of madness.

On Tuesday evening, Martin was not back from work when she had to leave for the opening performance. She prepared dinner for him, put Max and Lauren to bed and wrote a note to say she'd see him later. He hadn't phoned to wish her luck. The knife found her tender heart and pain mingled with the flustering butterflies in her stomach.

The atmosphere backstage was even more tense than the day before. This was the real thing. The second dress rehearsal had gone well and boosted their confidence but the nerves still necessarily jangled. Mary Watson, in particular, who had been quite calm, was fussing, moaning, and biting off the heads of the 'lowly' make-up girls and costume ladies. One girl got quite upset and was about to walk out but Rachel managed to calm her down and they laughed about 'the stupid cow'.

The lights in the auditorium went down and the intro music began. Then they were on, and apart from a few missed lines and the curtains jamming, it went very well and was greeted with loud, appreciative applause. Rachel's whole body sang with delight as she stood assimilating the clapping; glowing under the lights for the final bow. Then the curtains closed and they stood in blackness congratulating one another, waiting for the working lights to go on.

Most of the cast rushed off after a quick drink, it was late and a working day the following day. Rachel decided she wouldn't stay long either. She had parked her car at the back entrance near the stage door so she called goodbye to everyone, congratulated Nick and gave him a kiss, then left via the dressing rooms. They were in darkness, silent now after the earlier rush and buzz. The smell of make-up and paint lingered, she took a deep breath. As she was about to open the back door, she heard a movement behind her and then a hand on her arm. She jumped and turned to make out Gary. He took her hand and led her without speaking into the wings of the stage. His arms went around her and his head bent down, his lips met hers and she could not deny them. Her body seemed to melt into his and she floated into a golden light, spreading warmth and sweetness to her very being. His hands moved up to her hair and he kissed her neck, her cheek, her forehead, and then he held her face close to his and looked into her eyes.

'Why didn't you come?'

She sank down onto the floor and he knelt beside her stroking her hand, her face, she looked up at him in the dim light and began to talk.

Like opening a classroom door to let the children out into the playground, the words, and the emotions that had been restrained, controlled inside, came streaming out. She tried to explain clearly; she thought she had sorted everything out so distinctly in her head but as she told him that it was wrong, it felt so right. As she told him she wanted to stay with her husband and the children as a family, she wanted to stay with Gary. As she told him she loved Martin, the words sounded false and empty to her and she began to cry. Everything seemed muddled and contorted; all the nervous tension of performing, the underlying guilt, the worry for Jane, all came tumbling out, but she didn't tell him she loved him.

'I'm sorry. I'm sorry.'

'God, don't apologise' he said, 'I'm in the wrong. I thought we had something that you wanted. Life's too short. But I understand everything you've said and in a way, I envy you. Maybe Nina and I could have worked things out and had the strong bond that is obviously between you and Martin, despite problems.'

He held her to him and kissed her on the forehead. And oh, how she wanted to kiss him on the lips. And oh how her body yearned for his but she just nodded slightly, sniffed and managed a smile.

'Still friends?'

'Still friends, best of friends. Come on I'll walk you to your car.'

She got into her car and said she would see him the

next night. He told her she was superb and walked away. Every sense in her, every nerve strove to make her leap out of the car and run after him but she willed her hand to start the engine and drive.

Martin was not in when she arrived at the villa. She was relieved though he hadn't said he was going out. It was just coming up to midnight and it crossed her mind that he would have expected her later but she could only think of Gary and what he'd said and not wanting to face Martin she went to bed and cried herself quietly to sleep. What was going on?

Chapter 29

Kathy phoned the following day to invite herself over; to check on the tickets for the last night dinner theatre and to find out who was on their table were the reasons she gave.

'How's everything going?' she asked when they had sat down outside.

'Really well, I think,' replied Rachel.

'How are you feeling about it all?'

'I've been really nervous but at the end I feel marvellous, I'm thoroughly enjoying it.'

'How's Martin about all the nights out performing?'

Strange questions.

'Oh fine,' Rachel said and then regretted lying to her good friend. 'Well actually that's not entirely true. He seems to resent the whole thing. He's not been very supportive I must admit.'

'No. I got that impression the other night.'

'Oh, was it that obvious?' Rachel tried to laugh.

Ever the wise Kathy continued. She had never been one to not speak her mind, 'Is everything all right between you?'

'Not really,' admitted Rachel glad in a way that someone had noticed.

'Look Rachel. I love you and Martin and don't want to interfere but...'

Oh God, she knows about Gary' was all Rachel could think of. 'Someone saw us; someone's been gossiping'. That she should be the centre of the town's scandal and speculation horrified Rachel. She thought of all the affairs that had taken place in the time she'd been there. The awful gossip, the exaggerated stories from which she'd always felt removed.

'You had your dress rehearsal on Friday, didn't you?'

'Yes,' replied Rachel not daring to think about what was coming and not sure what Friday had to do with anything.

'Martin took the children out on the boat didn't he?'

'Yes, that's right, he went with a crowd from the sailing club.'

'Well, I don't think it was a crowd exactly.'

'What do you mean?' Rachel was now totally mystified.

'He took Tina with them. No one else.'

Rachel looked blankly at Kathy – nothing was sinking in.

'We came up to the beach he was on and, well, to be perfectly honest, Rachel, they looked closer than just friends.'

'What do you mean?' She needed it to be spelled out now, to be quite clear about what Kathy was actually saying.

'They were kissing for God's sake,' Kathy was getting quite agitated now at the seeming density of her friend.

'What?' she grappled to understand what Kathy was saying, 'But, the children were there!' This was not true; this was not happening.

'The children didn't see them, they were playing, oblivious to them and it is only by fluke that I saw it, they obviously thought they were hidden and as soon as we came round in front of them they moved completely apart. Look, I wouldn't have said anything if I wasn't sure and if I hadn't already had my suspicions. I don't like interfering but I felt, as a friend, torn between ignoring it or maybe trying to nip it in the bud. People have different views on whether to tell or not and I just felt I couldn't count myself a friend if I left it and you found out later, too late. You can hate me for it, but I take that risk.'

Rachel felt as if she had been kicked in the back and flipped right over. Memories of the warning signals came back to her, the whole train of thought that she'd been following concerning herself derailed. It was so completely ironic that she almost laughed but then she was overwhelmed by nausea. Taking Tina out with the children filled her with fury. But then, how could she talk?

She sat without speaking, waiting to feel something, think something, but she was numb. Kathy put her hand on Rachel's and told her that if she wanted to talk she knew where to find her.

Rachel pulled herself together and said, 'Thank you Kathy, I am glad you told me. You're a true friend. I'm not sure if it was the best time to tell me – God knows how I'll get through this show but well, yes, I shall certainly need you around, I expect.' She wondered whether to confide in Kathy, to tell her everything but decided she needed time to think.

'I am sorry to bring you bad news when the show is going so well but maybe there are more important things. I'll see you on Friday night – good luck.'

They kissed on both cheeks and Kathy left.

Kathy's parting comment was barbed. Rachel felt hurt that even she thought that it was because of doing the show that Martin had been forced to look elsewhere. She sat and stared ahead of her, thankful that Max and Lauren were both at a friend's house for the afternoon. She realised that she had been so wrapped up in herself and her own emotions, her own guilt and forced loyalty to Martin, that it had not crossed her mind that he might have found someone else.

And yet, that wasn't quite true, she had seen the warning signals but had not taken any notice. She felt hurt, betrayed, angry. Angry that she had struggled so hard against her feelings for Gary and that Martin had gone so far as to take Tina out on the boat with Max and Lauren. As she thought on, she realised she felt cheated. She had worked so hard at persuading herself that her feelings for Gary were wrong and that her marriage was more important. Now she felt she couldn't turn to Gary as she had made a choice against him and yet when she thought of him she wanted him so much. Maybe Kathy was wrong; maybe she was on the wrong track. As her thoughts were racing back and forth, the phone rang. In a dream, she went to answer. It was Martin.

'Hello,' he said.

'Hello,' she said.

'Hello,' he said.

'Yes?' she said.

'Listen, I'm really sorry darling but I've been told I've got to fly to Jordan. Something has been going on up there and I'm the only one who can sort it out.'

'Oh,' she said.

'I'm really, really sorry but it means I'll miss the show. If I could change it, I would.'

'Okay, don't worry,' she said automatically.

'Good luck, I know you'll be marvellous. I'll be back on Saturday evening and we'll go out for dinner.

You can tell me all about it, then.'

'Yes okay.'

'Look, there's nothing I can do about it.'

'No, no. That's fine. I'll see you on Saturday. Bye'

'Bye. Good luck again.'

She put down the phone, a huge, painful hurt gagged her throat and tears welled. She crumpled into a heap by the telephone table and sobbed. She didn't move for over an hour. She didn't know what to do, she felt as if she had been gazed on by Medusa, and turned to stone. But she had to move, had to function. Max and Lauren would be home soon. She had to get them ready for bed and then she had the show, she had to perform.

She rose in automatic, made a cup of tea, made herself move, and think about ordinary things. By doing this, she began to subconsciously analyse the phone call and to wonder whether maybe Martin was not going on the trip alone. It was a public holiday on Saturday and many companies and schools had taken Thursday off as well so that everybody had a long weekend. As she drank her tea and got things ready for the children, she wrestled with the growing temptation to find out where Tina was. The nagging thought got the better of her and she went through lists in their bureau of addresses and phone numbers. She found the sailing club sheet and Tina's number. Picking up the receiver, she filled with trepidation. As she dialled the number, her whole body began to shake. Somebody answered. She asked for Tina. The cheerful female voice at the other end told her that Tina had gone away but would be back on Saturday, could she take a message. In a falsely bright and casual tone, Rachel asked where she had gone. 'Jordan,' said the voice. 'Thank you' said Rachel. 'I'll call back on Saturday. Bye.'

Her whole body seemed to be in spasm, she put the phone down and put her arm out against the wall to steady herself. The doorbell went and she could hear Lauren shouting for her. Get a grip; she had to get a grip. She breathed in deeply and switched into Mummy before opening the front door.

'Hello darlings! Did you have a good time?' she said stepping outside. Lauren flung herself at her legs. Max wandered past her into the house. Rachel smiled at Lorraine, 'Hi Lorraine, thank you, were they all right?'

'Not a problem. They've had a lovely time and have eaten plenty so don't worry about feeding them.'

'That's great. Thanks. Would you like to come in?'

'No, I've got to dash, see you soon.'

'Okay, thanks again. Say goodbye and thank you, Lauren. Max, Max?'

Lorraine laughed and shouted bye as she left. Rachel got the children bathed and into bed and read them a story, externally loving and chatty, internally she was twisting apart. Luckily, they were tired out and fell asleep as she read. She closed the book, kissed them both and moved Max to his bed. Then she got ready, knocked on Junata's door to tell her she was going and left for the night's performance.

She blocked out everything and concentrated on getting to the Club and doing her part. Backstage she behaved as normally as she could and after a couple of drinks felt slightly calmer. In the wings, Gary patted her shoulder and wished her luck and she nearly lost control and dissolved into a soggy mass but kept herself and went on stage. Once again, it went down well. The cast were gaining more and more confidence and enjoying the whole experience. Rachel wanted to go straight home afterwards. She couldn't face Gary and could not keep up the external composure any longer. She was relieved that Martin would not be home, even though she knew what he was doing. All she wanted was to get through two more nights and then she could think straight.

As she tried to make a quick exit, she bumped into Nick, 'Rachel!' he exclaimed with a huge smile.

'Oh hello Nick – pleased?'

'Yes it really looks good and well done, you're really excelling yourself.'

'Thanks.'

'Dashing off tonight?'

'Yes, I'm so tired and I guess tomorrow and Friday will be late.'

'Are you all right?'

'Yes, why?'

'I don't know; you just don't seem your bubbly self.'

'Just tired I guess.'

'Let me know if you need a friend, eh?' He touched her gently on the arm.

'Thanks Nick, I'll see you tomorrow.'

'What a lovely man he is,' Rachel thought, as she got into the car and drove home.

She didn't find sleep easily. She was over the earlier wretchedness, but found she could not think straight about what was happening and what she was to do. Eventually exhaustion overtook her and she slept.

Chapter 30

Somehow, she managed to get through the next day and the performance in the evening. On Friday morning, she busied herself in the house. She wrote dutiful Christmas cards to friends and family pretending everything was normal, but actually thinking that they would be the last ones she ever sent with both her name and Martin's together.

In the afternoon, she took Max and Lauren to the ice-rink to avoid seeing anyone she knew and made it through to bedtime with a shard of invisible glass sticking out of her heart. She wondered how many of Martin's business trips had involved Tina. The number of times he had been away at the weekend or coinciding with school holidays. She knew she was going to leave him, but she also knew that Gary was not the answer either. She began to plan her alternatives.

On the way backstage, she met Kathy and George in the car park. 'Where's Martin?' asked Kathy perplexed.

'Oh, God!' said Rachel, 'I'm sorry. I should have let you know. He's had to go to Jordan.'

'On business?' asked Kathy.

'Hmm and pleasure,' retorted Rachel looking at her.

'Oh,' responded Kathy, for once she didn't know what to say.

'I'll see you after the show,' said Rachel turning off for the backstage door.

'Yes. Good luck,' replied Kathy, trying to keep the pity out of her voice.

Rachel felt strangely in control. All she wanted was to finish the show knowing she'd done well. Nothing was going to break her performance. The response from the other performances had proved that she could do it and she felt confident and proud of herself. She went on stage that night with a feeling that she wanted to show them all just what she could do. As all last nights are, it was superb; the audience was with them from the start giving the whole cast added zest and enthusiasm. The final curtain came and the crowd of friends and family gave them a loud, prolonged reception as they all came forward for bows. Rachel was given a bouquet of flowers and felt as though her heart would finally completely break as she realised she'd done it, and well. At that moment she ruled the world and could have done anything she set her mind on. Afterwards in the dressing room everyone seemed to mirror that mood. They were the best. It was going to be a good party.

Rachel changed and went through to the bar.

George and Kathy congratulated her, but couldn't stay as it was a private party. Kathy said she would call the next day and hugged her tightly. The Club had laid on a buffet and a disco was ready for after the usual speeches. The chairperson made a speech, Nick made a speech, and then the producer made a speech and everyone was congratulated and patted on the back. Presents were given and flowers handed out to the ladies' backstage. Everyone felt superb apart from the pianist, who had somehow been forgotten. There was a general flurry of apologies, and then miraculously another bouquet emerged from somewhere, so she was happy too. Then the music started and everyone high on adrenalin and alcohol threw themselves into partying.

Gary went up to Rachel and gave her a hug, 'You should feel very proud, you were excellent.'

She smiled and said thank you. She was overwhelmed with the urge to take him and hold him and kiss him and make love but he spoke, not looking at her, 'I called Nina earlier. I'm going to England for Christmas. We had a really long chat and I don't know, but I think we've got a chance of getting back together.'

Rachel's heart fell through the floor but she managed to say, 'That's great. I really hope it works out for you.'

'Well, if it does we've got you to thank.'

Rachel thought she was going to be sick. She made an excuse to go to the toilet and sat trying to control her burning, bursting chest and throat. She forced back the tears and reinforced her soul with steel, 'Fuck them,' she whispered to herself and returned to the party. Finding Nick, she proceeded to dance and dance. He made her laugh and she found she was actually enjoying herself, despite the constant need to find out where Gary was and what he was doing. He was talking and laughing with various people but she knew he was aware of her. Transparent strings attached them in an irrevocable bond.

Judy Tzuke's 'Stay with me till Dawn' came on and they automatically turned to each other. Rachel smiled and he came to dance with her. They held each other close not caring what anyone thought, their bodies seeming to mould together as one. Rachel wondered if she could say something but knew it was too late. As the last notes played out and faded into the next record, he held her away from him then drew her back in for a hug and kissed her on the cheek.

'You're very special, thank you,' he whispered in her ear.

'I hope it all works out for you,' she said. She smiled and hugged him and walked away.

Nick was at the bar in his cups, thoroughly happy. As she joined him and the group he was with, he put his arm around her shoulder, 'Here's my star.'

Rachel laughed and offered to buy a round.

'No, no I'll get this,' said Nick and proceeded to order a bottle of champagne.

A waiter filled the glasses and everyone toasted Nick and the show. He beamed with delight, 'All worthwhile in the end I suppose,' he said wryly.

Everyone started chatting or going off to dance and he turned to Rachel, 'Is everything all right? You should be ecstatic and there's something missing.'

'I am ecstatic,' she said laughing. 'I guess I'm just exhausted at the same time.'

'As long as you're all right,' and he put his arm around her shoulder. It was comforting and warm and she was grateful to him.

'I think you're gorgeous,' he said and she grimaced.

'No, I mean it. You've got so much to offer, don't waste it.'

She was close to tears so she suggested a dance. He readily agreed and they went up to join everyone else in a raucous accompaniment to 'Simply the Best.'

It was late, very late when she got home and she felt tired and drunk. She got into the empty bed and fell quickly asleep without time to examine the mixture of emotions that swirled and twirled within her including the dread of seeing Martin.

Chapter 31

She felt as if she'd been asleep for ten minutes when Lauren and Max jumped on top of her in the morning still in their pyjamas. She panicked thinking they were late for school and then remembered that it was a public holiday. She dragged herself up devoid of feeling and went through the motions of cooking them breakfast, taking them to the beach with Pinter and going shopping. Still unable to allow any thought she returned to the house and slumped on the sofa with Max and Lauren to watch The Little Mermaid. She felt her eyes getting heavy and drifted off to sleep. The phone woke her and she panicked about where she was and what time it was. Martin's voice brought her to her senses.

'Hello!' he said cheerily.

The hair on the back of her neck went up. 'Hello,' she said dully.

'How did it go then?'

'Very well, thank you.'

'You don't sound too pleased. Hung over, are we?'

He was so jovial she wished he were in front of her so she could punch him.

'Yes a bit. I was just dozing.'

'Late night then?'

'Yes, I think so.'

'Look, I'll be home about seven. Do you fancy dinner out?'

'Yes, that would be lovely.' She tried to hide the sarcasm.

'Right, see you later. Bye.'

She flopped back onto the pillow 'Bastard' she thought.

He arrived home with flowers and in a lively mood, 'Missed you,' he said as he handed her the flowers.

She could not believe this was the man she thought she knew so well. They went to the Mexican restaurant in the Sheraton, quiet on a Saturday night with the working week starting the next day. After ordering, she asked him how his trip had been.

'Oh, turned out to be a real fiasco but managed to sort things out.'

She watched his face, he could barely meet her eye as he described what had happened.

'How was Tina?' Rachel said sipping a margarita.

He looked at her and said, 'What?'

'You heard me. How was Tina?' She spoke calmly.

He stared blankly at her and for a moment, she thought she'd got it all wrong and was making a complete fool of herself but then he said, 'Oh shit.'

'Yes, oh shit.' She was unbelievably cool. She wasn't sure what she expected but it wasn't what he said.

'Look Rache. I'm sorry, but I've fallen in love with her. I didn't mean it to happen but you were so distant and then with this choral thing …'

'How long has it been going on?'

'I guess it started about a year ago.'

A year ago! She was struck by a thunderbolt.

'Just a bit of fun, not serious. You were always tired and distant and… I don't know things just sort of happened.'

'Not serious, not serious' she repeated in her head.

'So what's going to happen?'

'But I guess it just grew,' he continued on his own track.

Just grew. This could not be happening. This could not be true.

'Oh Rache, I don't want to hurt you. I love you and the children but, you - you just weren't there for me'.

'And Tina was?'

'Yes.'

'Tina who hasn't got any children. Tina who is free

and single and fun loving?'

He didn't respond.

'You pathetic jerk. Can she cope with two children?'

He looked up, shocked.

'No, don't worry. I couldn't leave the children.'

Rachel suddenly saw everything clearly. She probably had known, without consciously admitting to it. This was why she had been vulnerable to Gary.

'So you think it's my fault?' she asked him.

'No, I don't mean that. I didn't plan it. I guess it was separate. Separate from you and the children. Then, well the last few months. I don't know, you've changed. You've not exactly been the caring, loving wife…'

'You mean, 'good old Rachel's wasn't at your beck and call anymore. Finding your socks and pants, putting dinner on the table without question. Upset your perfect double life, did I?' Contempt and anger filled her. Her voice was getting louder.

Martin looked at her desperately. 'You weren't there for me and she was,' he said simply, his eyes unable to hold hers.

Rachel wanted to fight, shout, scream. She didn't care that they were in the middle of a restaurant. But, suddenly an overwhelming sadness filled her. What was the point in finding blame? She certainly wasn't blameless or innocent. It had all happened while they weren't watching. A stream of unconsciousness.

Intoxicated by sunshine and parties, an easy, comfortable life had lured them in and deceived them. They had forgotten to look after the little things, the important things.

It felt as though someone had snapped their fingers and turned her whole life upside down, but in reality, they were reaping what they had sown. Without realising, they had been wounding each other. Tiny, inconsequential grazes, if only they had tended to them. Left to fester and go sceptic, they had poisoned their love and their life together. In order to survive, the only solution seemed to be the amputation of divorce. Or was there still a chance?

'When were you planning to tell me – us?'

'Um, after Christmas. We didn't want to spoil the children's Christmas.'

'We' - it struck the final blow.

'That's very considerate. Smile and pretend we're a happy family through Christmas. Pretend to make love to me when you've just been with her and then drop the bombshell.'

'I don't want to hurt you or the children. I'll make sure you are all right.'

'He's thought this through, he has it all planned,' she thought to herself.

'I'll move into a flat with, with… You and the children can stay in the villa. We'll have them at weekends and holidays,' he paused to see her reaction,

'Don't be bitter,' Martin added.

'Bitter. Oh I'm not bitter,' said Rachel. 'I shall book flights home tomorrow. It will be nice to spend Christmas with Dad.'

'But, you'll come back?'

'I don't know.'

'But, the children....'

'I don't know.' Rachel stated, looking him straight in the eye. 'I think that's enough for now.' She stood up from the table.

'Rachel.'

She stood still.

'I'm so sorry,' he attempted and Rachel actually felt sorry for him. She walked out of the restaurant and headed for the Corniche.

A cool breeze swept across the water, chilling the tears that now poured down her cheeks. She walked without seeing. Streams of cars cruised along the busy coast road, a blur of lights and beeping horns to her left. The ruffled sea, silent and black lay to her right. She walked fast, head down, not knowing where she was going, ignoring the stares of passers-by. Arabic families out for an evening stroll. The men in crisp white kanduras, neatly folded headdresses held in pace by black circular agals. Their sons in miniature, identical kanduras without headdresses ran and chased each other across the grass and around the fountains. The women covered in black, constantly checking and redoing their shaylas to ensure they did not reveal their hair. Little Indian girls in bright pink frilly party dresses with huge brown eyes and long, dark, shiny hair, skipped and shouted, pointing in delight at kites flying in the air. Pakistani men walked hand in hand, their baggy shalwar kameez billowing in the wind. Filipinos in jeans and t-shirts laughed and chatted in high-pitched voices, and joggers plodded past in their Nike trainers and designer track suits. She was oblivious to them all.

She eventually slowed and paused to lean against the balustrade looking into the waters that had taken Sylvia without question. The moon, full and glowing shone benignly down, glittering on the surface, offering an illusory path of gold. She yearned for Gary to enfold her in his strong arms, but knew she couldn't go to him. She was glad she had helped to get him back with Nina, and wished him only happiness. He was not her answer. Nothing felt real. She could not think clearly, she just wanted to sleep.

She turned away from the moon and hailed a taxi. Arriving home, she was relieved to see that Martin was not back. She got ready for bed and went to sleep in the spare room.

It was a strange couple of weeks. Flights were full because of people going home for Christmas but Rachel managed to book her and the children onto a flight to Gatwick a few days before the end of the school term.

She knew she could keep busy with work, making costumes for school shows and taking the children to parties. While everyone around was in the Christmas buzz shopping and partying, she was packing and crying. She went round to Kathy's and told her what was happening. Kathy was very upset. Rachel and Martin had been very good friends and she was very fond of the children. She hadn't realised things had been going on with Tina for so long and wished she could have done something to help earlier. She met up with Gillian who sympathised and tentatively asked about Gary. Rachel found jaded relief in being able to talk about him and confessed all the details.

'I'm sorry. Sometimes these things work out for the best. I know that sounds crass and it's too soon to say, but you are young and attractive you will meet someone else.'

It was the last thing on Rachel's mind but she thanked Gillian for being a good friend and promised to keep in touch, if she didn't come back.

Jane was mortified and terribly upset that Rachel might not be around when the baby was born.

She told Abdullah that she needed to take time off and didn't know when she might be back in the country, so he should get a replacement. He didn't probe. He said that he would be very sorry to lose her. On her last day, he gave her a present of a small finely woven Persian carpet and wished her luck. Raju gave her a small pack of cinnamon sticks and said he would miss her.

Otherwise, Rachel told people that she wanted to go home and spend time with her Dad. Martin would be following. Nobody questioned it, but it wouldn't be long before the truth got round. She didn't care. Let them talk; entertain themselves with speculation and gossip. They would never know the truth, the real pain.

She knew she didn't love Martin any more, she didn't even feel jealous of Tina. He had changed. Without her noticing, the kind, gentle man had become hard; there was something almost arrogant about him. He had betrayed her and the children. This acknowledgement did not make it any less painful or sad.

She thought about Gary, but didn't see him or contact him. It was strange to think that he would remain a secret. There had been no reason to tell Martin, it would have seemed like tit-for-tat and as it was over before it had even really started, what was the point? She didn't know whether she felt sad about Gary or not. It had been wonderful and she felt inside herself they had shared something important, but she couldn't think about what might have been. Everything was too confused. She vaguely wondered what would have happened if she'd played it differently but stopped herself as she found herself missing him. Instead, she concentrated on her future in England sorting out practical issues with Martin in a civilised manner and planning what to tell the children. There was so much to do. Packing and sorting what to take and what to leave, in case they did return.

She took Pinter for a last walk along the beach. White clouds scudded across the blue and small waves crashed onto the shoreline. Saying goodbye to Pinter, not knowing whether she would ever walk him on the beach again really broke her heart, and she sat on a rock looking out across the channel remembering all the times she had walked this route, in particular the day she had determined to make things work with Martin. The pain in her heart and stomach spread up to her throat and she let herself cry, hugging her arms around her body, she sobbed like a little girl on the deserted beach, while Pinter huffed and snorted chasing different smells, his tail wagging.

In front of the children, she maintained an air of normality. As far as they were concerned, it was very exciting going to Grandpa's for Christmas, they might see snow.

The day came and she boarded the plane with Max and Lauren bound for London. She settled the children, fastened her own seat belt and stared unseeing at the TV screen in front of them. People were still boarding around her, putting bags into lockers and finding correct seats. She paid very little attention, and wondered whether she would ever be coming back to this weird and wealthy place. As the plane taxied and took off into the clear sky she felt strangely exhilarated at what lay before her. It felt as though she had been released from heavy, binding chains. She let out her breath in a huge sigh. Max and Lauren were busy searching through their packs of goodies from the airline so as soon as the seat belt sign went out she rose and made her way to the toilet.

She stood outside the engaged cubicle at the back of

the plane and gazed out of the window into the pale, endless blue. Suddenly, the reality of what was happening struck her with shocking force and the earlier sense of relief vanished. She was alone, a single mother with no plan, no fucking clue what she was going to do. Should she start again in the UK or should she swallow her pride and go back, so that the children could be near their father in familiar surroundings? Her stomach knotted in rising panic. A hand touched her shoulder and she shook herself, ready to turn and smile politely.

She turned around and gasped in surprise as she found herself looking into the face of Gary. Her stomach gave a leap of unexpected excitement and pleasure. She could not help herself smiling but then squashed the instinctive joy, as she reminded herself that he was on his way back to Nina.

'Hello! On your way to see Nina and the boys?' she asked forcing her voice to sound bright and off hand.

'Well, yes sort of?'

She looked at him quizzically.

'Well, they are expecting me – after Christmas. I – um – I only got this flight because I heard what happened and found out when you were flying.'

'Oh,' Rachel was still confused. 'But you and Nina, you are getting back together, aren't you?'

'No,' he said with a nervous grin.

'Oh – what happened?' she sounded concerned, although her true reaction was inextricable hope.

'Nothing. It was never a possibility.'

'But I thought, I mean you said...'

'I lied.'

Rachel stared at him, her mouth fell open and he smiled his wide, full smile that sent his face into crinkles. She continued to stare at him.

'I know you made a difficult choice with all the best intentions. I wanted you to think I was doing fine, out of the picture. I'm really sorry it didn't work out in the way that you wanted. Look, I know it's too soon, but I thought you might need a friend and well, just so you know, I'm here…'

She put a finger to his lips and said, 'You make me so happy.'

TO THE READER

Thank you for reading this story. I love hearing from you, so please contact me at:
sianscriptsinfo@gmail.com or on Facebook: Sian M. Williams

OTHER TITLES

INTO THE BLUE (Children's fantasy /educational)

EYES OF THE SOUL (Murder mystery)

DISCONCERTING SHORT STORIES

CALLING TIME (Romance)

THE HIVE THAT LOST ITS PURPOSE (Allegory)

PLAYS

WHAT HAPPENS NEXT? (Mystery ghost)

JOURNEY TO THE END OF THE RAINBOW (Fantasy)

CINDERELLA

SNOW WHITE & THE VERTICALLY CHALLENGED EXCAVATORS

THE CAMEL LOT & THE KNIGHTS OF THE DESK

RAPUNZEL II (Pantomime)

RUMPLESILLYSKIN

SLEEPING BEAUTY

Printed in Poland
by Amazon Fulfillment
Poland Sp. z o.o., Wrocław